Sharper Security

A sovereign security company novel by

Thomas Sewell

This is a work of fiction. Names, characters, places, and incidents either are the product of the author's imagination, or used fictitiously. Any resemblance to actual persons, or groups, living or dead, events or locales is entirely coincidental.

For a current list of books and short stories in the series, please visit SharperSecurity.com.

ISBN: 978-0615730073 (Trade Paperback)

Published in the United States of America

Catallaxy Media, Phoenix, AZ
http://CatallaxyMedia.com

Dedicated to my wife, for all her love and support.
Spring is coming and she is the master gardener,
Of my heart.

Contents

Historian's Introduction

They called it the "Big Split", when the United States of America were united no more. East and west coast states went their own ways. The old south and the corn states stayed about as they were, poorer than the rest, but trying. The northern Rust Belt states looked inward, fighting to hold on to what little they had left. It was the western states, tucked away from the moderating Pacific Ocean, that made the biggest changes. Texas, Utah, Idaho, Wyoming among them, but especially the newly formed Arizona Zone.

As a historian, I look for the threads that turn into the fabric of history's fate. The conflict of Sharper Security versus Policía La Raza is one of thickest of those threads. Ultimately, it helped shape how an important part of the post Big Split world turned out. Below is the story of the beginning of that conflict. One day in France, and then much later, a single week in the Arizona Zone, was everything required to spark a much larger fight for freedom.

Justice became swift in the new Arizona Zone.

Prologue

Rue Roulle, Paris, France

In The Near Future

Evie jumped in her seat as Pierre slammed open the door of the parked surveillance van. "Wrong apartment!" Pierre shouted. In contrast to his typical French countrymen, Pierre always seemed to be shouting. "Evie, you must stop them!"

A Friday afternoon, cloudy and quiet. Wiping sweat, Evie thought the summer air was a little more humid than usual. She took a breath and frowned at Pierre, wondering how his iconically long flowing hair managed to stay dry in the heat and humidity, "Looks like it's getting ready for another downpour. Lucky I brought my brolly in with me today." She half lifted her umbrella to show him.

"There is no time!"

Stop everything now? Was he kidding her? Twenty-eight years old, two years into her job with Special Branch, Evie sensed Pierre and the rest of the local Gendarmerie Intervention Force resented the command of a foreigner, especially a young *English* foreigner. Despite their attitudes, Evie Martin was determined to ace her first field assignment and make South Croydon proud.

"Close the door, Pierre." She scanned monitors showing the breaching explosives attached to the apartment's door and the nearby hallway walls, "We've been tracking this couple for weeks. Calm down. There's loads of weekend traffic comin' soon. We can't wait longer to capture them, they'll be awake soon and the tourist events they're targeting start tomorrow."

Pierre stepped farther into the van, closing the door behind him, "We were wrong. It is not them. Someone else must be using their computer remotely."

Evie flipped her blonde hair nervously, and then gestured at the screens showing men in Groupe d'Intervention de la Gendarmerie Nationale uniforms clearing the locals out of the neighborhood, "Too late to stop without botchin' it. The charges are set. We have our orders and approvals. Everyone is almost clear. The go order was given from the highest of levels only ten minutes ago."

"I have irésistant évidence! During zee attempt to change de train route, our surveillance shows personne à la maison, ah, no one was home. They are, in short, a decoy." Pierre's words tended to become tangled by his excitement.

"Or accomplices... It's too late for 'em, anyway." Didn't he understand she'd received final official approval already? The men were in place. The new entry procedure she'd proposed had been blessed. How would it look if she called it all off at the last minute? It would take days to get multi-government approval again.

"But ..." Pierre's response was interrupted by a faint shock wave pressing in on them. A monitor showed the door and walls exploding inward just before the roar of sound reached them.

"A clean job." Evie nodded towards the screen, satisfied. "Only the one apartment touched, no damage to the neighbors. All appropriate regulations followed."

Pierre seemed stunned, "Too much force. That is not how it was to be."

It was later, when Pierre was picking through the destruction looking for more evidence, he heard the baby's muffled cry.

"Quel désastre!" Pierre exclaimed. *What a disaster.*

Chapter 1 - Day One

18 Years Later

Cowtown Road, Casa Grande, Arizona Zone

Early Afternoon

Sam Harper wanted the four prisoners safely behind the walls of his Sharper Security prison. No matter how friendly their relationship, he became nervous any time his job required him to spend time in another sovereign security company's headquarters. Too exposed.

Sam reached down for the hundredth time that day to hitch up his utility belt and tuck his khaki uniform shirt farther into jean shorts. The pistol, ammunition, security and communications equipment on his belt weighed heavily. Someday he'd find a properly fitting belt for his height. Until then, he resigned himself to use adjusting his clothing as an excuse to consider his surroundings.

The plush, soft décor in the office of Agence de Sécurité contradicted the message of four prisoners in strictly functional restraints along the inside wall. Sam didn't have to clean the place when blood was spilled, but at least the furniture looked like it could be wiped down.

Sam glanced over at Pierre, the former Frenchman, and his son Edmond. The two of them stood safely behind the plate glass protected counter of Pierre's sovereign security company.

Pierre is always so much more stylish, Sam observed to himself. Junior Agence personnel, including Edmond, wore matching blue berets, tight uniform shirts and creased blue pants. Pierre made an exception for himself on the beret. Sam imagined it didn't fit his long hair very well. The Agence de Sécurité's office walls featured Impressionist prints under soft spotlights. Sam preferred Romanticism.

Sam listened to Pierre continue describing the four prisoners, watching them from behind his computerized sunglasses. He dismissed the first two prisoners as nonentities. They weren't going to be any trouble. The third was small, but glowering fiercely. Must think he's important.

Pierre wrapped up his description of the third prisoner, "Shortee Tejada has an attitude. He's uh, overcompensating for his La Raza Council parentage. His papa is une personne importante. My son Edmond's first arrest. Decent golf swing."

Sam noticed Edmond smile when his father mentioned the arrest and Shortee's golf swing. Must be something there. Edmond's hand brushed the butt of his holstered pistol, and then jumped a bit as he realized his motion could be seen as a threat. He casually moved his hand up to grasp a large silver cross hanging from a chain around his neck and made sure it stayed there in plain sight.

"What's this last one in for, Pierre?" He gestured towards the tall, muscular Pima Indian in his early thirties, long raven hair pulled back in a ponytail. Looks experienced with violence, Sam thought. Definitely put that one down first if the prisoners start something. Might be good on the prison football team, though.

Pierre pushed back his hair with his hand and called up a file in the display in his glasses, "John Wild Horse Parkur, he stole an autocab on the I-11 toll road near rue Casa Blanca. Drunk and disorderly. En accord, ah, stipulated to petty vandalism and disturbing the peace. His Father is a judge for the Gila River Rez. Agreed to pay restitution to the complainant in addition to 90 days in your lockup. Scar on his left wrist." Pierre blinked while focusing on the send button in his glasses, "I'm forwarding ze full file now. Edmond's second arrest."

Sam looked over the group of four men in utility hand cuffs and robotic leg restraints again, wrinkling his nose a little at their smell before directing his comments to Pierre, "Glad to hear you fellas are setting new records. Doesn't Agence de Sécurité make your prisoners bathe anymore?" He loved giving Pierre a friendly jab and the Agence usually smelled more like a French café than a carnival ride.

Pierre looked embarrassed, "That uh last one threw up in our holding cell, twenty minutes ago. Edmond barely had time to help him change before you arrived. Ze Agence doesn't have robotic guards and automatic wash-downs like your cozy air-conditioned facility." Too right, Sam thought. Not many sovereign security companies around here could afford what Sam could in terms of equipment. One of the reasons he stayed on top. Well, that and his pricing.

Sam blinked at the text displaying in his sunglasses, "I've forwarded Sharper Security's acceptance of the prisoners as well as the indemnity bond details for keeping them stashed away. As usual, a pleasure doing business with you." He turned towards the four men, gesturing towards the door with his hand pressing the unlock button on a key fob, "Your leg-irons are unlocked so you can walk now. The van's outside getting hotter by the minute, so let's go." Have to be firm with prisoners, especially at first.

Pierre said, "Things are better now that we have the contracts for toll road security and the Francisco Grande Sports Complex. Having Edmond old enough to help out doesn't hurt the bottom line." Sam knew Pierre wasn't getting any younger. Good for him to have an apprentice, especially his son.

Sam watched John glare at Pierre and Edmond, and then shuffle resentfully out the glass double doors to the parking lot surrounding the tan stone building. Definitely keep an eye on that one.

As the other three prisoners followed John, Sam waved to Pierre and Edmond, "Someday you small timers are going to build your own long term storage and make us catch more of our own prisoners, but for now, thanks again for the business."

"As always, a pleasure." Pierre said. "Ze Agence won't cross you as long as I am chargé d'agence and Edmond is no more fool than I."

Out in the parking lot, Sam let the prisoners file into the back of the black and white mini-van and then hit the lock button on the key fob, freezing their leg restraints. "You fellas are either rich or lucky. Most of Pierre's prisoners end up in that hellhole of pink tents out in the desert. We keep it at 68 degrees inside our place. Out in tent city, you're lucky if the open air showers are that cool." Sam glanced around the parking lot, making a mental note of the vehicles. Always useful to keep track of the world around you.

Sam climbed into the driver's seat and looked back through the security glass to the rear compartment. "Not very talkative, huh? Well, you're lucky I was coming through Casa Grande today to investigate a preacher's piano theft. Otherwise you'd have had to wait for the regular weekly transport bus, which isn't nearly as comfortable as this van."

Looking across the road and nearby railroad tracks, out over the open Sonoran Desert to the south, Sam quoted a different Frenchman's description of the area to himself. Granitic sand pierced in a thousand places by primitive rocks, appearing like the bones of a skeleton whose flesh is partly consumed; A wide land covered by irregular masses of stone, among which a few plants give the appearance of a green field covered with the ruins of a vast edifice.

Driven by Sam, the mini-van with a "Sharper Security" logo on the side started toward the Maricopa - Casa Grande Highway. Sam set the autodrive to take him back to the Sharper Security prison and began reviewing the new inmates' files in his sunglasses. He needed to get the four prisoners processed and into their new prison routine fast enough to not be late for his dinner with Maria.

Elliot Road, Mesa, Arizona Zone

Evening that same day

Evie was exhausted after traveling halfway across the world in a fast jet plane. Over here, they used big drop capsules attached to parachutes to land passengers along the plane's route. Back in England, they actually landed the airplanes.

When boarding the plane, they'd strapped her and the other nineteen passengers destined for the Phoenix area into five rows of seats within the same drop capsule. As the pilot announced the plane was approaching the release point for the Williams Dropport, the adrenaline of anticipation shot a burst of energy through her.

Oh, they said it was safe enough based on passenger miles fallen, but while actually dropping through the sky with nothing but a big silk parachute keeping you from plunging to your death, it didn't seem very safe to Evie.

All twenty passengers made it down alive, with only a soft bump during touchdown. With the relief of landing, Evie's exhaustion took over again, deeper than before.

She directed a rolling luggage carrier to her reserved autocab and curled up in the back. The consular notary and party supply store she wanted was only eight minutes from the Williams Dropport, but Evie dozed off anyway during the drive.

Evie woke up to the ding of the autocab stopping at the curb and highlighting a building on the right in its window display. She felt emotionally drained, but it was time to officially register her arrival and finalize her property purchase.

She was grateful for the widespread availability of self-driving vehicles. The traffic she'd seen scared her. Oh, the speed and density wasn't much different than what she was used to near London, but everyone here drove on the wrong side of the road! She was sure she'd cause an accident if she ever had to drive herself.

Despite the periodic dust clouds, the roads were wider, straighter and smoother here in Arizona than Evie was used to in Britain. Not as cold in the evening, either. Something to be said for the desert. The roads had a lot more trees than she'd imagined. There'd obviously been a lot of planting and watering over the years.

Evie ducked out of the autocab and primped her hair once. She dug around in her bag for a makeup applicator. No sense in not using any lingering advantages. After a second to touch up her makeup, she was ready to dazzle. Maybe whoever ran the store would hook up her up with something special. A bright neon light over the entrance flashed "Eurotrash" in stylized lettering.

She stepped through the entrance and peered around. No attendant. There must be a mistake. The land registry required you to show up in person to sign certain documents in Arizona Zone. What's the point of having to sign things in person if you weren't going to meet with someone? Does anyone even work here?

The gaudily decorated store held a series of large booths. Several booths appeared occupied, legs showing below curtains, any sound from inside dampened. Evie guessed she was supposed to just pick a booth. So much for smiling her way into a favor. The Americans she met back home always claimed service was worse in Europe, but how could it be much worse than a self-service booth? Back home, at least you could do this sort of thing online. Maybe customer service became worse after the Big Split. She shrugged.

Ducking inside a booth, Evie found a padded seat and a large screenpad with the words "Welcome to the Eurotrash Consular Notary and Party Supply Store". Prominent sections of the screen for Consular Services, Notary Services and Party Supplies invited her to press them. The latest release from *Cracker's Back* started playing softly in the background as she sat. Really? She had to show up in person just to use a touchscreen computer?

Judging by the amount of screen real estate devoted to it, they seemed to be pushing the party favors pretty hard. Must be tough to make a profit on that when you could just pick up whatever you needed online any time you wanted. She guessed that needing notary services must be a good indicator you had something to celebrate. Otherwise, the pairing was odd.

A few Consular related touch screen pushes later and Evie was officially diplomatically checked into Arizona Zone from London. That was the easy part. Now to finalize the purchase of her new home. It wasn't a mansion by North American standards, but it was incredibly bigger and nicer than she'd ever be able to afford in London on her retirement pay. You got a lot of house for the money in the City of Maricopa. Located on the outside of a sharp curve in Cartegna Lane, the rear yard was huge. Perfect for a garden, she thought. Widowed and 48, she planned to have some fun while she still had her youth.

Pulling up the document reservations for her new home in the notary section, there were too many options, most without any default choices. Brilliant. Only the roads and security sections were required, though. She sketched a question mark over the road options, looking for explanations. How complicated can buying a house be? Road options? What the 'ell?

After concentrating on reading for a few minutes, she interpreted them to mean she wasn't allowed to buy property without some way to be sure she could get to it. That idea just confused her more, "How could you not get to your home?" She finally just picked the cheapest option, "One road company share – local access – up to two concurrent vehicles".

Under "Security Services" Evie didn't even bother to read the explanations again. She'd heard tales about the Wild West, but was it so dangerous you were required to sign a security contract? Don't they have police here? Fancy civilization much? The cheapest "Standard – Response and Representation Only, No Pre-Existing Conditions Covered" still looked expensive when compared to her fixed retirement income.

With inflation, 20 years of civil service work didn't provide much, especially after the August Unison Riots in London. She needed to live on twenty-five percent of her London salary. At least there weren't any taxes here. That would help. The VAT was a killer back home. You could get a great "no rain" deal on a home in Arizona, as long as you didn't terribly mind leaving your mates behind to rot in London's wet weather.

Moving out of London was a good idea. Evie didn't need to remember her late husband Hamish every time she ran into one of the couples they knew. Her old friends tried to set her up, but hadn't the foggiest. Looking for new fun in the same places Hamish took her to wasn't going to work either. Best she get a new start in a new place. An adventure. What was that old saying, "Adventure is what happens to someone else far away?" Well, she was now that someone else, far away.

After another 15 minutes of drawing initials and signatures on the screenpad, Evie's arm was knackered. She rubbed her right elbow, glad to be finally done with the paperwork. They should call it screenwork instead.

The sellers required an identity guarantee bond and even the cheapest bond agents had a requirement to show up in person at a certified facility to sign everything. A lot of bother for nothing. With video spoofing, how could they actually prove it was her in the recording anyway? Check autocab records for the location and time period? Really quite stressful. She was glad the rules were old-fashioned when she'd been charged with enforcing them.

Evie signaled for another autocab on her phone as she left the booth. Time to look at her home in person.

He lay on his back in bed and stared at the information displayed in his glasses. She was here. She'd just purchased a house. It seemed petty, but the only thing he could access right away was her new trash pickup service. He put in a cancellation notice and wondered how long it would take her to figure out they weren't coming. He shivered in the heat.

Rita Road, South Tuscan, La Raza Council

Late that night

Lieutenant Garcia of Policía La Raza woke up with a start, his snoring cut off by an insistent buzzer. He sat up in his office chair and pushed a button to connect the video call, "Aló? Duty officer speaking."

The fancily-dressed mayordomo for Victor Tejada appeared on the screen, "Shortee Tejada has gone missing. Su padre is concerned."

Garcia shook the cobwebs out of his head, "Again? Did he wander off from another party? Where did they last see him?"

The mayordomo failed to look amused, "He was staying at a hotel up north, the Francisco Grande. We haven't heard from him after last night."

Garcia's next question was obvious, but he wasn't awake enough to assume the mayordomo wasn't a fool. "Have you tried calling him directly, or the hotel?"

"Sí. Not unusually, no answer from Shortee. The hotel simply states that they do not provide information about their adult guests." His voice implied Garcia should know that the mayordomo for such a powerful man would be at least somewhat efficient at his job.

"Policía La Raza is on the case. We will locate him and ensure his safety as a courtesy to Señor Tejada." Also, to save our own skin, Garcia left unspoken. An opportunity for positive or negative notice from his superiors.

"Gracias. See that you do."

So, the big man wants Policía La Raza to exert some influence on behalf of his son to get him out of yet another mess. Garcia pulled a beer out of the mini-fridge nearby. Better make some calls. If necessary, maybe bring Pedro's squad in on this. Pedro sometimes had an bad attitude, but he got results.

Another fine day in La Raza Council.

Chapter 2 - Day Two

Hidden Valley Road, Maricopa, Arizona Zone

The next morning

Waking up in a prison dorm room sucked. The air conditioning *was* nice, though. Place was clean, too. John noticed big water nozzles sticking out of the walls at regular intervals. Guess the inmates weren't relied on for *all* the cleaning in dorm #4.

There were a couple of things John "Wild Horse" Parkur knew after growing up Judge Parkur's kid. Prison sucked and the Judge was going to be more than a little upset the next time he saw him.

He still wasn't sure how he'd managed the tactical acquisition of an autocab while drunk out of his mind, but then he didn't remember much about the last couple of days. When he was in the Corps, John was never much of a liberty risk. Nobody liked to talk about it, but even his sainted Great, Great Uncle Ira, Famous Pima Indian, tied one on once in a while. He'd found out Ira never went to college either, even if they did name the high school in Bapchule after him.

They'd called it a medical discharge and disability from the Corps, but it wasn't just John's wrist. With another surgery, they could've fixed the bone spurs that made him unable to rotate his arm completely. Watching Marko and Cockbay, two of his closest buddies, turn into vacant meat on a useless training mission. That was worse than prison.

John stood up and picked his way through the maze of metal bunks with sleeping inmates. Right now he just needed to use the head at the end of the room.

Just before he got to the doorway, he managed to kick someone's bunk. John mentally damned himself and winced at his headache.

The bed's occupant stood fast enough it was obvious he hadn't been sleeping, "You gotta problem, fish?" This guy barely came up to John's shoulder. The French guy yesterday called him Shortee. Probably not wise to use his name.

He tried to be tactful, "No Sir, just clumsy this morning."

The five foot inmate glared. "Where'd you learn to walk, ese? Oh wait, obviously you didn't."

John started considering which was the best kneecap to kick first.

"You think because you're big and dumb, you can disrespect a man's bed? Te voy a filirear." *I'm gonna stab you.*

John stayed silent, daring him to start something. Prison fights never ended well even if you won. The guards made sure of that.

"Maybe you should crawl from now on? Be safer for all of us and you won't bump your head. Not that there's much to knock around up there, eh, ese?"

Obviously, this guy was looking for a fight on his first day. Maybe he was trying to establish a reputation by taking down the biggest of the new guys. Time to try a distraction. "You ever been to 29 stumps?"

The brief confusion on the guy's face at the question was classic, but the freezing high pressure stream from water cannons hitting them both in the back of the head surprised John almost as much. He'd thought the big hose nozzles sticking out of the walls were for cleaning. Obviously dual purpose. His mistake.

After being knocked over by the cold water spray, the eight legged robots wrapping his arms and legs in zip ties to await a human guard seemed anti-climactic.

John sighed. He still needed to hit the head.

Sam glanced from the monitor screen hanging on the wall back to his desk. In every batch, there was someone with something to prove.

He liked his desk. Obsolete? Sure, but he liked having drawers to put things away in. A nice clean desk top was a thing of beauty. If paper was out of style, a clean desk was probably the only stylish thing Sam had ever done.

He'd release the new prisoners from their zip ties in a bit. Sam found that laying in cold water for ten or twenty minutes could be very beneficial to one's attitude towards one's fellow prisoners.

A small video feed of Hidden Valley Road, running past the prison's narrow private driveway, unexpectedly appeared in the corner of his glasses. Sam instinctively tensed for an attack in the split second before the video was accompanied by the words "Personal vehicle of Judge Parkur approaching. Estimated arrival, 6 minutes."

Sam knew he'd have to deal with the Judge about this sooner or later. Sooner had arrived.

He stood and started making his way across the prison compound toward dorm #4. Better to release the new prisoners now. Who knew how long Judge Parkur was going to want to talk about his son John.

Cartegna Lane, Maricopa, Arizona Zone

Same Morning

Last night, Evie'd carried in only enough of her possessions to get some sleep. She thought about having some food delivered to procrastinate a bit longer, but decided she'd better just get started. Sooner begun, sooner finished.

Evie stepped outside her home and looked around for the first time in the daylight. The road ran at right-angles to her driveway. All these old tract houses, why are they all painted in dirt colors? Could use some bold reds and blues to spruce up the place. Everything blended in. More trees than she expected in the desert, though. Some of them thirty years old, giving plenty of shade.

All the nearby homes, including hers, had a small yard sign for "Sharper Security" with contact info. A package deal in the neighborhood, she supposed.

The big sheet metal shipping container with all her possessions looked out of place at the curb near the end of her driveway. Evie wheeled the unpacking robot from the back of the container and unfolded its arms. Her huge home had a master bedroom upstairs over the garage, another two smaller bedrooms, two loos, a living area, formal dining area, kitchen, even a laundry room. She'd taped pieces of paper with numbers on the walls that matched the numbers on the boxes inside the shipping container.

Shouldn't take the unpacking robot long to carefully empty all the boxes along the walls of each room. Evie's gardening equipment would all go in the back of the garage near the door to the outside. What little remained of her husband Hamish's things could go in the garage also. She could feel waterworks threatening at the thought of going through what she had left of Hamish. Still too soon. She'd save dealing with that for later, when she might be feeling a little stronger.

Evie started the unpacking robot going, and then led it on a familiarization tour of her home. After that, she could leave it alone and try to keep up with placing everything just so. Long days ahead, but in the end she'd have a real home. In a couple of days, she could relax and start looking for some of that adventure she'd promised herself.

He woke up after sleeping in. Had to pull a double shift last night. Time to see if the aerial drone he'd redirected from the standby flight was overhead yet. He started humming a classic tune by *The Police* under his breath.

Ah, perfect. Already in place while he'd slept. He made the video feed from the drone available in his glasses. Wasn't modern technology grand? He played back the last few hours the drone captured and watched as she walked around the outside of her home, finishing using a robot to empty a storage container. Hmm... she needed to pay, but how to start?

Ah-hah. He started work on the command and control systems for one of Maricopa's local autocab franchises, overriding some of the safety code with an emergency priority. This was gonna be good!

Hidden Valley Road, Maricopa, Arizona Zone

About that same time

Sam met Judge Parkur at the north gate into the prison, next to the small visitor parking lot and narrow private driveway. His scanners said the Gila River Pima judge wasn't carrying any weapons, "Morning, Your Honor. I suppose you've come for visiting hours."

Judge Parkur smoothed the lapels of his light grey Italian suit coat and struck a pose exuding patience, "Sam, you've known me a long time. Do you think I'd consort with the criminals you warehouse here? I'm here to talk to you about the case of one of our tribal members. He hasn't had his full contractual rights afforded him."

Sam took that sort of language personally and couldn't help taking a jab himself, "Criminals like your son, I suppose?"

Judge Parkur's smile started looking strained, "As the Chief Judge for the Tribe, I'm not used to people talking back at me. I suppose you think I should get off the Rez more often."

Sam sighed. Clearly, Judge Parkur was worried about his son and not used to having to negotiate when it came to the law, "Well, come on in to my office and let's talk about John's contractual rights." If there was anything Sam knew better than man's potential for violence, it was modern contract law after the Big Split.

Sam led Judge Parkur through the empty exercise courtyard, past the dorms and up to his office. Sam gestured him to a seat in front of the desk, and then instead of sitting behind it, pulled up another chair in the front of the office to put the judge at ease.

Judge Parkur started right in, "I'm forwarding you and Pierre a proclamation of jurisdiction from the Tribal court for John. I'm his father, so of course, I wasn't involved, but John is a landholder and official member of the Gila River Reservation and entitled to the appropriate protection. Under our general contract with Agence de Sécurité, John is entitled to a hearing in front of a Gila River Judge." Not unusual. Generally, in cross-jurisdiction cases like this, the offender's sovereign security force would insist on its own trial, if only to preserve its reputation for protecting its members.

Instead of going to war, sovereign security forces usually had a contract with each other. Contracting either directly or via intermediaries, interlocking contracts allowed for peaceful resolution of jurisdiction disputes. Nobody wanted to go to war over a petty criminal. Too expensive. "I'm surprised you're here and not talking to Pierre. Sharper Security is just a subcontractor in this one 'cause Pierre doesn't have the room to keep anyone in his lockup more than overnight. It's a revolving door over there, but most of his cases just involve restitution and punitive damages, so he doesn't have much need for long term storage."

"As I said, I'm also sending the proclamation to Pierre to start the clock on the agreed time frames in our contract, but you're a key to this as well. If John is declared innocent by a Gila River Judge, it won't be anything more than most will expect, but it's not going to overturn the Agence's decision in the case. Once we have two conflicting judgments, it goes to arbitration before a neutral third judge to receive a final decision both sovereign groups agree to follow."

Sam wasn't sure he liked where Judge Parkur seemed to be going with this. It might cost Sharper Security payments he was currently entitled to. He called up the file summary in his glasses, "Wasn't much of a decision for the Agence to make. John stipulated to petty vandalism and disturbing the peace. Didn't dispute the arresting officer's account. Not much evidence needed to be provided. Pretty clear the events happened on the I-11 toll road, well within Agence de Sécurité jurisdiction. Video evidence from a drone and the autocab itself confirm the officer's account."

"If a Reservation judge finds John innocent.... then it can only create bad blood. If the neutral judge finds John guilty, it'll look like my influence is the only reason it went to a third judge. If the neutral judge finds John innocent, the Pima People may start taking a dimmer view of the I-11 toll road company and the security they've hired. Maybe dim enough to start something, as most of I-11 runs through the middle of tribal land."

"I'm sure you're about to get to why you're here instead of discussing all this with Pierre." Sam said, even though he had a sneaking suspicion he was about to get pulled deeper into the whole mess.

Judge Parkur smiled, "It seems to me that we could clear this whole mess up a lot faster if we knew ahead of time how the neutral third judge would rule on the case. Pierre could unilaterally drop the charges, or the Rez could join with Agence de Sécurité's verdict. Either way, save everyone a lot of time and money, not to mention reputation and possible ill feelings."

Sam decided to jump ahead of the judge. Might as well meet your fate head on, "And Sharper Security, being local and large enough to enforce any binding arbitration on either of you, happens to typically be the first choice for a neutral third judge for both Agence de Sécurité *and* the Gila River Reservation. You know we get paid well in order to provide third party arbitrations, don't you?"

"I know it costs the Rez a lot of money in lawyer and witness time to put on a trial back home, then turn around and defend the results all over again in front of a third judge." Judge Parkur drove the final nail in, "I spoke to Pierre on the way over here. Agence de Sécurité is willing to skip all the expense and accept whatever Sharper Security decides after reviewing the evidence. He'll convince the management of I-11 that he's saving them enforcement costs and he trusts you to do the right thing."

Sam cut to the inevitable, "I want our usual hourly fee for arbitration and I want it understood that Sharper Security will decide based on the facts, which won't necessarily match what John's father may wish them to be."

Judge Parkur managed to look slightly offended, "That's all I'm asking. A fair look at the case and save us all some trouble. Pierre will cover half the arbitration fee. Of course, if John doesn't have to serve out his current sentence, Pierre won't have to pay you to house him for another 89 days, but I'm sure you'll be fair." He stood, "Thanks for your time. Please let me know the results once you work things out with Pierre."

Sam couldn't help but grin as he showed him out. Gotta hand it to the judge, got everything he wanted and made it sound like he was doing everyone a favor along the way. Time to start reviewing the evidence against John in detail.

Cowtown Road, Casa Grande, Arizona Zone

Late afternoon, that same day

Pierre stood behind the counter at Agence de Sécurité, talking on his video phone to well-fed Lieutenant Garcia from Policía La Raza, "Again. He is no longer here for you to come take. He is remanded to Sharper Security custody. You may threaten all you like, but our contract with ze Francisco Grand Hotel requires Agence de Sécurité to apprehend and hold miscreants who damage hotel property and injure guests."

Lieutenant Garcia scowled closer into the camera, face blocking Pierre's view of his Dos Equis enhanced belly, "We are your close neighbors to the south, Señor. You would do well with our cooperation in Policía La Raza matters. Then we could provide warning if we hear things about the businesses and homes under your protection."

It would be just like La Raza to send some of their hombres out to cause trouble where ze Agence would be responsible for the damages, and then disclaim responsibility later. One last try to talk sense into them. "We have your La Raza member on video knocking golf balls from the balcony of one of the tower penthouses, trying to hit their baseball bat shaped pool. Three women in the pool area and one man on the sidewalk were injured before our officer arrived and stopped him. I don't care how importante his papa is in your community, nor what party office he holds. When Monsieur Shortee Tejada has completed his sentence, he will be released. Not before."

The video screen went blank as the Policía La Raza Lieutenant disconnected. Pierre decided he'd better move some Agence de Sécurité officers toward the more southern areas he covered, especially around Casa Grande and towards La Raza Council territory in Tucson. No sense in not being ready for trouble if El Barrio Punks in Tucson were encouraged to head north and make trouble. Taking Lieutenant Garcia's implied threats seriously, he'd have to use some of the spare drones to cover ze northern end of Agence territory instead of the normal patrol cars.

Hidden Valley Road, Maricopa, Arizona Zone

Early evening, that same day

John came in from the exercise yard to find one of the spider guard robots waiting for him in the dorm, repeating "Follow me, John Parkur" over and over. He could really use a shower first to cool off, but whoever sent the robot wasn't likely to be patient and he preferred to avoid showering the hard way again. His buddy Manuel wasn't going to ever need a shower again, so John didn't feel like complaining. If fate had it in for him, well, fate missed him by a couple of feet last time and would just have to aim better next time.

Following the robot guard, John made his way through the prison to an office with an enormous desk magnified by how little it appeared to be used. Behind the desk stood the tall man he'd met the day before, again in khaki uniform shirt and jean shorts. "John Parkur, reporting as ordered, Sir." Old habits die hard.

"Have a seat." Sam said, gesturing to a chair in front of the desk. "Former Marine, right?"

John picked a different chair in front and sat down. "Oorah."

"Sam Harper. If you didn't catch it, I run this place. I need you to tell me what happened when you were arrested. I'm looking into the case at the request of your father, to make sure everything was done properly."

"I am taking responsibility for my inability to handle my drink, Sir. I copped to the charges, no need for a trial. No desire for a trial." No one would be able to say John Parkur didn't take his punishment like the best of them.

"That's commendable, but while justice can be swift, it still leaves me with some questions about what happened the other night. You don't appear to have anything better to do at this time than satisfy my curiosity."

No apparent way out. John still wanted that shower. He'd try to keep this interview brief, "Yes, Sir."

"Let's start at the beginning. On the night you were arrested, when did you start drinking?"

"Two, maybe two-thirty in the afternoon. Went to that Irish Pub in town."

"How many drinks? What time did you leave?"

John was already sick of answering questions. Why drag his lack of control out again? He leaned back and folded his arms. "I no remember, white man. I drink 'til drunk, waitress order me a cab, I wake up with that frog cop's kid shining a flashlight in my face. Go watch the 'tube of it online."

Sam stared at him for a minute, and then abruptly said, "You don't actually remember, do you? Alright, that'll be all. Follow Robbie here back to your dorm."

John stood and hesitated, and then walked out after the robot. Tired of this man's world anyway.

He watched her through the eyes of the borrowed surveillance drone, catching glimpses through unshaded windows as she moved from room to room placing things just right. He wasn't normally allowed to use the infrared cameras on the drones, but as the light faded, he turned them on to keep track of her as she moved around the second floor of her new home.

She moved into her bedroom over the garage and started hanging outfits in her closet. Women always loved enormous closets. How many clothes could one person wear, anyway?

Either way, she obviously planned to be at it for a while, so a good time to put his plan into motion. He continued working on the safety and control systems for the autocabs, using the override he had in place. He hummed to himself as he worked, the back of his mind smiling.

Just as he finished the reprogramming, he lost his video feed from the surveillance drone. Had someone discovered his illicit use of the drone? Was someone on his track?

Someone tracing his actions? Did he trigger an alarm?

A quick check turned into a sigh of relief. The drone he'd appropriated as a spare had been recalled for use elsewhere, along with the other spares. A coincidence that it was needed while he was using it, that's all. It made his work more difficult and less enjoyable, but he'd be able to work around the loss and watch through the cameras on the autocabs.

He began guiding them into place now that their safety interlocks were compromised. Twenty-seven should be enough to ensure maximum destruction. That's all the company had available, anyway. At least, without complications from passengers. By the time anyone noticed an unusual number of autocabs circling the area looking for fares, it would be too late.

Hidden Valley Road, Maricopa, Arizona Zone

Evening, that same day

Sam stepped from his private stairwell into the underground garage below his office in the Sharper Security prison. His arrival triggered indirect lighting to fill the spacious cavern of vehicles. He liked to patrol the local area personally and make sure he still had a feel for the communities he protected.

A set of tall thick steel garage doors on the North side connected the cavern to the road outside. Always use the right tool for the job, Sam thought as he looked over his choices in the garage. Lined up against the south wall he could choose from a utility pick-up truck, a prisoner transport minivan, a standard police cruiser, a Land Cruiser and a restored and upgraded Corvette. All the vehicles were painted police-style black and white and prominently displayed the Sharper Security logo. The pick-up truck looked like a workhorse compared to the sleek lines of the Corvette, while the Land Cruiser appeared ready to climb the nearby black stone ridges.

The west side of the garage contained a mechanic's lift with an assortment of tools hung on the wall or stored under workbenches. The east side had an open spot reserved for Sam's armored assault vehicle. Need to get that back from the weapon smith, he thought. Changing out the rear machine gun for a rocket launcher shouldn't take them that long.

Sam smiled at the final vehicle, a long semi-truck and trailer painted white taking up the space along the edge of the east wall. Not much to look at, Sam knew the normal looking exterior concealed reactive armor and an assortment of weapons ports. A holdover from the early days after the Big Split, when truck-jacking was a popular sport, before all the new political arrangements were sorted out. Sam had fond memories of the look on a truck-jacking crew's face when they realized the truck full of luxury goods they thought they were hijacking was actually a mobile fortress.

Similar in concept to the old Q-ships of World War II, decoy merchant ships used to lure in enemy submarines before revealing their true warship colors, Sam's semi-truck and trailer didn't get much use anymore. Not many people dumb enough to try to hijack a truck in an era of panic buttons and fast-responding road security teams.

Today, like most days, Sam felt like driving the Corvette. Fast and retrofitted with a suite of modern electronics, complete with a missile launcher attached to the roof. The prison's garage door barely moved out of his way as he sped out his private driveway to Hidden Valley Road.

Sam flipped on the transponder in his black and white Corvette to let the various road owners know he was driving on business. The transponder also told his dispatch office he was patrolling and available for calls. He turned right from Hidden Valley Road onto old highway 238 and mashed the gas pedal to get up to his standard cruising speed of 113 mph. His Corvette's radar system showed only a few cars on the road, plus the gliders landing at Estrella Sailport north of 238. Even with a rare bit of traffic, he easily reached 113 well before passing the old junkyard and the Rez's golf course.

Putting the Corvette on radar cruise mode toward downtown Maricopa, Sam called up the footage of John's arrest in his glasses. Something didn't add up. How did John supposedly take over the autocab while lying drunk in the back seat? Edmond's arrest report suggested John cracked into the controls online before climbing into the back seat, but to Sam he seemed a bit too wasted for that level of critical thinking. Maybe this kid John was a superstar with control systems who could break into an autocab's wireless dispatch system and steal it while blind drunk, but nothing in his Marine service record indicated more than someone good in a fight.

John seemed more like the type Maria, the woman who ran the home for children from war torn countries Sam sponsored, would want to take in. Tough, but a little broken and in need of some understanding.

As Sam passed into the outskirts of the City of Maricopa, Barro's Entertainment Metroplex glittered ahead on the left. Sort of a young Italian's dream world, complete with pizza, rock bands and rollercoasters. Maria hated it, preferring to cook industrial size meals at home rather than spend the money to go out, but the kids in the orphanage loved it.

Expanding the children's home Maria ran for him was expensive. Still, Sam could certainly afford an occasional trip for all the kids to Barro's. War orphans don't live on bread alone. Sometimes they need circuses and rollercoasters.

When Sam's Corvette reached the overpass across John Wayne Parkway, an incoming video call from Pierre displaying in his glasses caught his eye, "Evening, Pierre. What can I do for the Agence?"

"Ah-hah, tonight it is what can ze Agence do for you. We have a short subcontract available, if you would like. Some, uh, lowlifes out of La Raza Council are rocket racing down I-11 and ze Agence autos are too far south to be there soon enough. Your dispatch told me you are three minutes away."

While Pierre spoke, Sam accelerated to 220 mph and checked to make sure his Corvette's active jamming and anti-missile defenses were online. "I'll take it on our standard terms, including any ammo expenses or damages covered. Send me the drone feed."

As usual, Pierre was fast and efficient. Video feeds from a pair of Agence de Sécurité surveillance drones popped up in Sam's windshield heads-up-display (HUD) within seconds. One showed a long distance camera shot of the fronts of two long low rockets on wheels, complete with cockpits and black paint. The other showed the giant rear nozzles of the land rockets. In both, Sam could see the macho crowd finishing preparations and holding back a line of cars.

"They are standing around for five minutes now, but will not last." Pierre said.

Sometimes Pierre's French accent was difficult to understand, but Sam got the gist of it. They won't be standing around long, if they've ever done something like this before. In Sam's experience, gang bangers from La Raza Council had plenty of experience making trouble for peaceful citizens. They probably monitored Agence patrol cars to figure out when the northern end of the high speed toll road would be clear of law enforcement. Too bad for them Sam wasn't as far away. "I've got it. Thanks, Pierre."

"Best of luck to you, Sam. They cannot be scaring the paying customers."

Sam made a smooth left turn transition from Highway 238 onto the wide, eight lane toll road and watched in the HUD as groups of bandana-wearing men around the now visible two land rockets began to scatter to the sides of the road. "Understood. Looks like they're about to light those things off. Wish they'd keep this crap out on the salt flats."

Traffic was already backed up down the toll road from the blockade ahead, so Sam slid out into the left shoulder of the freeway and turned on his visible and audio emergency signals. All the nearby drivers would be warned to move out of the way and anyone on auto would reliably move aside as well.

With a good two miles to go until he reached the start line for the drag race, Sam popped off a pair of electro-magnetic-pulse (EMP) missiles and sent them shooting ahead. With luck, he'd be able to disable the land rocket vehicle's electronics before the fireworks even started. Sam understood the desire to build a land rocket and race it, but not why these thugs couldn't be bothered to do it on their own property, instead of trying to appropriate a toll road meant to be used by long range cargo haulers and short range citizens trying to get home from work as fast as possible.

A flashing alert from the Toll Road management popped up in Sam's HUD, "Warning, heavy traffic ahead! Emergency response vehicles en route." No kidding.

One road rocket clear of the crowd must have seen either Sam's Corvette or the EMP missiles coming, because it looked like a second sun rose right in front of Sam's eyes. His glasses auto-shaded to compensate for the glare of the single rocket firing, but that made the rest of the scene almost too dim to make out.

The lit land rocket accelerated away just before the pair of EMP missiles detonated over the crowd and the remaining rocket. Not only wouldn't that second rocket be going anywhere, but anyone in the crowd without military grade shielding was going to find it hard to make a phone call or send a text. He could pick them up at his leisure. Even La Raza Council criminals weren't suicidal enough to walk into the surrounding Gila River Reservation lands without an invitation. They'd pay a lot more for trespassing on tribal land, without any sympathy for their ancestors not being among those who started the grudge.

Unless he waited for it to burn out, which wasn't exactly stopping it, Sam's Corvette wasn't going to catch a land rocket traveling almost 500 mph. In the next few seconds of the rocket's acceleration, he had to do something. Usually these racers waited until they blocked traffic on the road long enough so their path was clear for miles ahead. Firing earlier than the racers planned, it was likely the guy trying to steer it would drive it right into the back of a cargo hauler creeping along on auto pilot at only 90 mph. With the weight distribution of the rocket designed to keep it from leaving the ground, and the speed it was traveling, it was likely to flip any car or truck it collided with right off the ground and kill the passengers. Sam couldn't let that happen.

Cartegna Lane, Maricopa, Arizona Zone

About that same time

Evie finished unpacking her clothes into her closet and decided the toiletries in the loo could wait. Time to curl up in a nice soft bed with her favorite blanket and get some sleep. Plenty still to do tomorrow. What's that roaring sound from down the street, Evie wondered. Sounded like several cars gunning their engines. Don't they have noise ordinances here?

Before Evie could investigate the sound, the first autocab impacted her garage door with a loud crash and a thunderous crunch. Evie's bedroom shook as two more impacted the sides of the garage below her. She screamed. She tried to rush toward the center of her home, away from the edge, but was knocked off her feet by the impact of three more roaring monsters into the walls below.

Lying on her gasping diaphragm, trying to catch her breath, Evie stared at the carpet grain in front of her. You could tell what path the vacuum took and where she'd walked afterwards by where the carpet showed a bit shabby. How to get away? She tilted her head toward the doorway out into the hallway and possible safety. She must move. Left arm, right leg. Trembling limbs. Right arm, left leg. Must keep moving, gobsmacked as she was by the continued impacts below turning into a slow roar in her ears.

She heard a groaning and wasn't sure if it came from her lips or the building around her. Right arm, left leg. Past the end of the bed, closer to the doorway. Another impact below. Clinging with white knuckles as the floor tilted outward below her with a collapsing sound. Another impact farther away. Left arm, right leg. More movement underneath. Sounds of sliding and crashing.

Left arm, right leg. Right arm, left leg.

Pain broke out of her left side as a nearby table lamp shattered while partially impaling her waist. Never liked that lamp anyhow. She touched her left side and winced in pain. Her fingers coming away bloody. The floor began to disintegrate around the edges of her vision. Is this what it was like for her husband, Hamish? Did he have time to think of her at the end? Right leg, left arm. Keep moving. Blood on the carpet doesn't matter. Panting is ok. Left leg, right arm. Oxygen is good. Smells quite dusty in here now. Must breathe.

Evie's right hand reached the doorway into the hallway. A nice three level design on the door casing. A child could have their finger pinched on the hinge-side. She'd considered children. Perhaps a boy and a girl. Left it too late. Really quite stressful raising children while working in the Home Office. Left leg, right arm. Move. Hamish understood. They needed, well, could use, the income and she needed the people contact. Hamish always did protect her from herself. Right leg, left arm. Keep moving, slowly, but must keep moving.

Lean up a bit, compensate for the tilt of the floor. It's just a struggle, children and work. Evie was absolutely devastated when her best friend had a child. Hardly ever saw her again. She struggled to a crouch, using the door frame as a crutch. Pulse pounding. Use both trembling feet to launch into the hallway. Run hard. Must breathe. Push out the arms and grab at the air to go faster. Pump her arms just like her constabulary training.

Floor wobbly from the continued impacts below. Nothing solid. Run down the second floor hallway. Dusty again. Crashing below. Groaning above. Need more oxygen.

See the cracked window at the back of the house. Second floor isn't that high up. Getting lower by the second. Glance back. Quite the pileup of autocabs out front, all hammered into each other and into the garage. Turn toward the already breaking window. Tilt body for impact. All of Hamish's things down in the garage. Likely completely ruined. All she had of him.

Launch with the legs, shoulder leading. Crash. Cuts. More blood. Free-fall. Hamish would be so pleased with her, so pleased. Impact. "Huuuuoohhhh". Dirt and sand. Just lay here. Really quite stressful. Close eyes. Rest. Fade.

He continued accelerating each autocab in turn, watching through their navigation cameras as they crashed into the house or into the autocabs preceding them. Despite how the short street limited their acceleration, he was happy with the damage. Without the drone's overhead view and infrared sensors, he couldn't see exactly where she was, but he cut through most of the front of the house, using autocabs like arrows. Cutting out supporting walls, robin hooding one cab into another to push it further into the wreckage, making sure no part of the house reachable from the street remained. See how she liked being on the other side, being the target.

He still had a few arrows in his quiver. He could hear the crashes through the microphones used by the autocabs to listen to passengers. The pile-up in front of the garage was several cars deep now. He wouldn't be able to push those much more into the house. He sent cars into the block walls on either side of the house's front yard. He sent more into the space they cleared, caving in each side of the house.

Firing more autocabs into the middle of the pile, he finally exhausted his supply. From what he could tell, the house was destroyed beyond repair, at least 80% collapsed. A good day's work. She couldn't be indifferent anymore.

Listening to the few still functioning autocab microphones, he heard emergency vehicles arriving. Probably an ambulance and several Sharper Security cars. He should disconnect and wipe any records of his override so they couldn't trace him. He knew what to do from his practice run.

Hmmm... She likely wasn't dead. What to do next? Perhaps arrange a dose of the pain he'd lived with while she gallivanted about London?

Rita Road, South Tucson, La Raza Council

About that same time

Lieutenant Garcia, candidate for either division Captain or traffic Sergeant in Policía La Raza, depending on how this matter of Shortee Tejada ended, swirled his open beer bottle and scowled as he watched the Agence de Sécurité forces movements on the large touch and video screen table. The expert computer system tracking and interpreting their movements for him was top of the line. Almost as nice as those available to the Underwriters who stood behind most of the security contracts in the Arizona Zone. Agence de Sécurité had most of their borders with La Raza Council well covered. Pierre might be getting old, but he hadn't built up el Agence by not anticipating opponents.

Garcia felt secure in his top floor office. The solid stone three-story fortress Policía La Raza built to house their headquarters didn't have too many offices on the top floor and Garcia pulled many strings over his career to get his. Most of the men in his special operations division worked out of an old wooden barracks near the edge of the chain-link fence surrounding the ten acre property, but as a trusted Lieutenant, Garcia rated his own office. The perks of being on top were generally pretty nice, but they also came with responsibility to very demanding superiors. Men had been executed for failing to please some of Garcia's superiors in Policía La Raza.

Time to update his immediate supervisor and supreme leader of the special operations division, fearfully and affectionately known to his men as el Jefe. He wasn't going to be happy. Garcia finished up his beer and set the empty bottle out of camera range.

Lieutenant Garcia placed the call, opening up a window in the corner of his tabletop touch-screen for the video, "Compañero Jefe. I must report that our ploy failed to achieve the desired results. Agence de Sécurité hasn't opened up any holes in their patrols to respond to the rocket drag racers. I don't know why yet, but I will find out. This is only a slight delay. I am sure we can achieve the penetration necessary to reach the target very soon."

Garcia tried to suppress a wince as the Policía La Raza Jefe responded, "Victor Tejada calls me every hour to demand when we are going to get his son out of the hands of that gabacho prison. Remember that Victor Tejada es muy importante member of the Council. The same council that pays your salary and lets you make a fool out of yourself every Saturday night with the Señoritas. Do something about it. Soon."

Garcia replied, "Sí, el Jefe. We don't have the forces to cut through Agence de Sécurité quickly and then take on Sharper Security with enough force remaining to be back to La Raza land before they are able to bring in one of the Underwriter's ready response divisions. If going in hard only cost lives, we could still consider it, but we would lose, and lose in such a way that Councilperson Tejada's son Shortee would die in the operation and start an unbacked war in the process."

El Jefe wasn't in the mood for excuses, "Make it happen."

Garcia cringed. Time for some realism. "A war we would lose, el Jefe. We are superior to them all, but there are many more of them and they don't share with the poor like La Raza, so their soldiers are much richer in equipment. The only way to have a chance at a rescue is to get significant force past Agence de Sécurité and close enough to the Sharper Security prison to hit them with surprise and then fade safely back into the desert. The land rockets didn't work, but we will work something out. It just takes time."

"If Shortee Tejada is still in prison at the end of the week, you will receive similar accommodations here in La Raza. Keep me updated on your progress."

"Sí, el Jefe." Lieutenant Garcia said as he disconnected. Traffic Sergeant was starting to sound better and better. Now he needed to figure out how to get Shortee Tejada out of prison without starting a war where the defense companies backing up the contracts between sovereign security companies stepped in on the other side. That's a war Policía La Raza would lose, with literally devastating results.

Time for another beer before placing a call to Pedro.

I-11 Toll Road, Gila River Rez, Arizona Zone

About that same time

Raoul Dominguez finished writing his trip report in the cab of his 42 wheel truck. More like a road caravan. The rumble of the road passing beneath the wheels distracted him at times. He preferred listening to music. At 90 mph, 25 more minutes to the warehouse in the west valley, and then he could unhook his three big trailers, turn in the report, and head for home. He hadn't been home in three days, running a round trip to Miami and back. Even with the customs stop in Pensacola on the way out, he'd made good time.

For the millionth time in his driving career, Raoul glanced at the identification transponder at the top of his windshield. He still wasn't completely sure how it worked inside the small plastic case. Somehow, all the roads he drove on were able to ask from a distance which truck it was attached to, match the encrypted identification up with ownership and payment records in a database and charge him for his road usage. Not only no slowing or stopping to pay tolls, but he could download a printout of his usage anytime he wanted. That, plus his charge account with the major fuel sellers, made it easy to fill out the cost portion of his trip report.

His profit was whatever remained after collecting payment for the trip, minus an allowance he saved for maintenance costs per mile. Running his own truck took a little more paperwork than being just an employee, but Raoul thought it was worth it for the control it gave him over his own life.

Of course, it helped that he was really on board for decisions, emergencies, and paperwork. The computers did all the actual driving. If the driving computer broke, he was pretty sure the first sharp turn would defeat any attempt at manual driving. He may own the big 175 foot cargo hauler, but it drove itself. Each trailer's wheels had to be controlled individually in real time in order to corner within a reasonable distance.

After three days, he missed his wife, his media naranja, *better half*. He made a mental note to see if she wanted to go with him on his next long trip.

The roaring of the land rocket caught Raoul's attention before he actually saw the speck in his side mirror. The speck became a distant black rod with fire blowing behind it. Madre de Dios! There was no way he could get his truck out of the way of that thing before it destroyed him.

If he survived the crash, his wife would kill him! Not only that, he'd be ruined. Even if he managed to make the road owners pay for the damage to his truck and cargo, he'd still have to earn back the trust of people who expected their loads to make it on time and without incident. The worst would be if he was hurt too badly to keep working. His friend Steve used to own his own truck, until he had to give it up after breaking his hip in an accident. What would his family do? Madre de Dios!

The firing land rocket continued to rapidly approach as Raoul crossed himself and said a rapid Hail Mary over an imaginary rosary.

Sam's Corvette roared past the defunct land rocket, focusing on the one quickly getting away. Even at his Corvette's top speed of 220 mph, the black land rocket had accelerated enough to start to pull away from him. That much mass times acceleration was tough to stop.

Continuing his pursuit, Sam glanced at the feed from the Agence drone showing the rocket rapidly approaching the back of a long haul truck, with Sam's Corvette pursuing. That truck was probably the slowest of the vehicles that came by just before the banditos blocked traffic. Time for some assistance. He touched a control to reconnect with Agence de Sécurité. "Pierre, I need full control of your drones. One of the rockets is escaping and about to catch up to some traffic ahead on the road."

"You have it." Pierre replied, as additional steering and other aerial drone controls added themselves to the image in Sam's HUD.

Sam flipped his Corvette back on auto, telling it to maintain maximum speed on the same course. He'd only get one shot at this and he needed to concentrate.

He guided the drone lower. Sam knew that in order to keep from lifting off the ground, land rockets were built nose heavy. That also generally allowed the rockets to plow through anything they hit, but only if the front of the rocket got under it.

He dropped the drone even lower, trying to line it up right in front of the still accelerating vehicle. Land rockets are not the safest form of transportation. The driver is normally wrapped in a cocoon of steel composite with a pressure suit and five point harness protecting him from the effects of a crash or explosion. The safety measures also limited the driver's visibility. With limited visibility and without a clear roadway, there was no way the rocket would dodge all the traffic ahead. These hombres sometimes had problems just staying on the road, even eight lanes wide.

Just as the nose of the rocket was about to intersect the camera on the drone, Sam dropped it down and to the left, flying the drone into the ground just ahead of the front-right wheel well. The camera feed from the drone went out, but Sam watched through his windshield as the bump under only one side of the rocket shifted its center of gravity to the left side. With barely enough weight to keep the nose down under full acceleration, that was enough to lift the rocket in a half circle to the left, causing it to start sliding along its left side.

Unbalanced and no longer rolling on wheels, the exhaust starting demonstrating that the body of the rocket wasn't as tough as the surface of the road. Pieces peeling off and the rocket starting to turn towards the edge of the road from the uneven drag, the driver reacted quickly and cut the fuel. Even then, Sam watched the rocket turn sideways to the road with much of its original momentum intact. The land rocket started rolling sideways so quickly it was difficult to tell exactly how many times it flipped before coming to rest.

Sam spoke again to Pierre as he decelerated, "We're going to need an ambulance for this one and the paddy wagon for the others I left behind, but we'll have traffic moving again for most lanes in about ten minutes. Going to take a while to clean up the rest of that rocket and clear the other lanes, though. Better have toll road maintenance dispatch a robot cleaning crew with a dump truck they can load up. Sorry about wasting the price of a drone. You owe me for two EMP missiles and some gas."

"Merci, Sam. You've helped more than you know."

A second video feed from Sharper Security's dispatch computer filled a corner of Sam's HUD, "Subscriber injured by attack. Please divert to Cartegna Lane as soon as possible for non-emergency crime scene analysis. Estimated travel time, 12 minutes."

"Pierre, we need to talk about one of Edmond's arrests, but I have another call to take. We can talk a little later. I'll stay with the driver and render first aide until the ambulance arrives, then lock down those spectators involved so they will stay put until your paddy wagon can grab them, but the paperwork will have to wait. One of my neighborhoods has had some sort of attack, and if it was just a dog biting a man the dispatch computer wouldn't have broken through in the middle of something like this."

"I understand. Ze ambulance is on ze way. Fais gaff! Policía La Raza may try something soon to release Shortee Tejada. Bonne chance." *Watch out. Good luck.*

"Thanks for the warning. We'll talk later." Sam disconnected the call to Pierre as he parked his Corvette next to the largest still intact piece of the land rocket cockpit. He pulled up the video feed from Cartegna Lane in his glasses as he stepped out to see what aide could be rendered before the ambulance arrived. He hated multi-tasking like this, but it looked like he had two large wrecks on his hands.

Porter Road, Maricopa, Arizona Zone

Later that night

He turned on the car light in his Camaro and stared at his quick notes about Flag Health Center. Parked in their parking lot, the front of the wide square white building looked just like their image online, perhaps slightly older. Hopefully the online floor plans matched as well. He'd been busy researching ever since she was taken there. He had access to the all their regular public information online, plus access to the identities of their patients and assigned room numbers. No way to control their care from his online access, though. At least, not yet. What he needed was to plug something into their internal network.

He removed a small cube from his pocket and stared at it. A complete network relay in an inch square box with two Ethernet connections. The connections showed on opposite sides of the cube, one male and one female.

He pulled up the hospital's patient list again. Perfect, a maternity patient in the process of checking out. Room C3. Different ward, but on the same floor she was on. With a little luck, close enough that the medical devices in the birthing room would be on the same local network as the medical devices he needed to access.

Popping the cube back into his pocket, he stepped out of the Camaro. Closing the black car door behind him, he headed for the main entrance, putting a big smile on his face.

He strode confidently through the front automatic doors and into an elevator to the maternity ward. The secret is looking like you know what you're doing and where you're going. Looking lost or confused just invited questions or attempts to help. Conversation could lead to suspicion. Nope, just another visitor who knows his way around and exactly where he's going.

Once upon a time, a receptionist or nurse might have watched him enter and questioned his presence, but in today's automated hospital, where half the staff worked remotely and never stepped foot in the place, they didn't have those kinds of bodies to keep watch in person.

The cameras high up on the walls saw him, but he didn't look out of place. Births were sometimes last minute unplanned affairs. It wasn't unusual for someone new to arrive to the party, no matter how far along matters were. Most people held their birth somewhere more relaxing, like at a spa, or at home with telepresence bots representing hospital staff at the right time, but many were still comforted by being in a hospital with additional emergency care right next door. A certain percentage of pregnancies were considered high risk and planned to be in the hospital. Others became high risk and were rapidly moved there before proceeding. He planned to take advantage of the presence of one of those.

It wasn't his first time checking on an emergency birth. Glancing at the rooms down the hallway, he could tell which were occupied by the light shining out through square cutouts in the doors. The occupied rooms would be locked and he'd be unable to enter without identifying himself.

A pair of men lingered next to a long window in the hallway, presumably staring at fresh babies. No entrance there without interrogation and authorization from someone on duty remotely.

He picked room C3. The patient he'd identified earlier was already checked out, so no need to identify himself. He verified the lights were out and strode in. Quickly moving to one wall, he removed the Ethernet plug from a monitoring device, inserted the male plug on the cube from his pocket into the wall and the Ethernet plug from the monitoring device into the other side of the cube.

No more than five seconds later, he was back out in the hallway. If anyone was watching, it would just look like he missed the patient, arriving too late for the release after the birth. He shrugged for the cameras benefit, glanced at his phone and then headed back to the elevators.

Time to go home and get back to work on getting control of the right medical devices for her room. Hopefully he'd finish before he had to go back to his regular job. This was like working two jobs, but the satisfaction paid for the effort.

Chapter 3 - Day Three

Cowtown Road, Casa Grande, Arizona Zone

The next morning

Pierre stood behind the counter at Agence de Sécurité, talking on his video phone to Sam Harper from Sharper Security. "With de bruit, uh, ze noise La Raza's been making, I'm short-handed up north. Thanks again for taking the subcontract and dealing with those road rockets last night."

Sometimes Pierre thought westerners had no sense of style. Sam looked ridiculously underdressed on the screen, wearing jean shorts as usual, with only a grey t-shirt. "No problem. Glad to handle it. With Sharper Security growing, I don't get to take my own car out for a ride often enough lately. I'm calling because I've had time to review the evidence in the John Parkur case. Judge Parkur told me you were willing to abide by my findings informally, without invoking contract rights and getting the Rez court system directly involved."

If only Pierre could transplant the western sense of justice back where the cuisine was sophisticated. Of course, if there was justice in France, he'd still be living there. "That is correct. Agence de Sécurité will abide by your decision in the case. Ultimately, that would be the result of the formal contract process anyway. What have you found?"

Sam frowned, "Bad news, I'm afraid. I know it's one of his first solo cases, but it appears Edmond screwed this one up. John was obviously drunk and belligerent, so the disturbing the peace charge will stick, but based on the evidence, I don't see any way he could have stolen that autocab. Not while drunk, not from inside. In fact, he appears to be passed out when it happened. At least based on the video feeds from the toll road cameras, from what I could see through the back windows."

Pierre mirrored Sam's frown, he wasn't happy about accusations of incompetence, "Someone took control of that autocab from the company's dispatch. The record is clear on that. They lost control of ze autocab and Edmond spotted it weaving all over the road."

"I know, but it wasn't John Parkur. It appears he was just taking the autocab home when someone took it over from the outside. I know no one else was nearby, so it was a reasonable assumption that Edmond made, but John doesn't have the kind of background where he's capable of breaking into an autocab control system while faking being passed out." Sam replied, "We know he was actually drunk while interacting with Edmond, based on the blood test administered, but where's the direct evidence tying him into the autocab theft? The video Edmond took clearly shows John not reacting well to being rousted ..."

"He practically assaulted Edmond." Pierre interrupted.

"... but without the theft of property charge, he doesn't deserve the sentence you gave him."

"Very well. It sounds like you've made up your mind on a judgment." A judgment I'm obviously not going to like, but Edmond is still young yet, Pierre thought. Vous pouvez compter sur ce qu'il dit; il appelle toujours un chat un chat. *You can trust what he says, he always tells it like it is, calling a cat a cat.*

"I have. I've sent you the file so you have a paper trail, but in essence I'm going to leave the fine for drunk and disorderly, but exonerate him for the theft and associated prison time."

He must really think John's innocent. If John hadn't originally agreed he was guilty of the charges, this information would have come out in a trial. Surely more John's fault than Edmond's responsibility. "The prison time the toll road is paying Agence de Sécurité for, which we're in turn paying you for?"

Sam sighed, "If we kept in jail everyone who might make us a little money, we'd be banditos with a kidnapping racket, not sovereign security companies our customers look to for justice and protection."

"Ah, tu m'étonnes, tell me something I don't know."

"I'll make sure John doesn't end up with hard feelings. I may be able to make up some of those lost prison fees in the process. We'll see."

That's the Sam Harper he knew, always looking for a way to turn a situation around for a profit. "Bonne chance."

Hidden Valley Road, Maricopa, Arizona Zone

A few minutes later

A spidery guard robot interrupted John's dice game in the dorm, repeating "Follow me, John Parkur" over and over. He glanced at the pot, took one last throw and then collected what remained of his winnings. By the time he got out of prison, he might have enough to finish paying off his debts. It's not like the debts were huge and these guys were neophytes compared to the crap games he used to run in the Marines while ship bored.

John stood and followed the robot, "I'm coming, Robbie. No need to nag."

He made his way through the prison and back topside to the same office as his previous interview, and then gave a mock salute to the occupant in shorts and a grey t-shirt, "John Parkur, reporting as ordered, Sir." He took a seat without an invitation this time. Maybe it'd get him kicked out without having to suffer any more questions. He didn't think the guy who ran the place would want to spray water around his own office, but he casually looked around for water nozzles anyway, just in case.

Sam smiled, "I have good news for you. I've reviewed your case and with the concurrence of Agence de Sécurité you are being exonerated of the autocab theft charge. As a result, your prison sentence has been reversed and you are free to go. The Agence will keep the fine you paid for the disturbing the peace charge."

Great. His Father the Judge tries to ride to the rescue again. Not this time. "I prefer to serve out my sentence and take responsibility for my actions."

Sam looked incredulous, "You prefer to stay in prison for a crime you didn't commit?"

"How do I know I didn't do it? It's all a blur. Besides, I like it here. Good air-conditioning. Frequent showers. Pleasant company." John grinned. Let's see how he takes that.

"You have some enemies out there I don't know about, that you'd prefer to stay away from?" Sam asked thoughtfully.

"Nothing like that. Just prefer to be responsible for myself."

You could see the light go on in Sam's eyes, "This wasn't Judge Parkur spreading influence for his son. Contractually, you were entitled to a review of your case by a third neutral sovereign security company. This is the result of that review. You were passed out in that autocab. No way you stole it. Technically, someone else stole it and kidnapped you, but that's Agence de Sécurité's problem to figure out."

John shrugged, to explain he wasn't moved by the appeal.

Sam looked a little cold, now, "You appear to be questioning my sense of justice. You aren't responsible, because you didn't commit the crime. You don't have to go home, but you can't stay here."

John tried a different tack with a little more intensity, "I had to borrow the money for the fine, and it's not like I had a whole bunch to start with. I don't know if you noticed, but Marine Corps disability pensions aren't exactly being kept up to date by anyone anymore. Since the Big Split, most jarheads hired on with local private companies or one of the big defense firms, but who wants to hire an officially disabled drunk and disorderly ex-Marine fresh out of the brig and pining for his lost comrades, Sir?"

Sam laughed and started smiling again, "I thought you'd never ask. The point is, I would. Do you want the job?"

What? Not the reaction John was expecting. He thought for a second, and then replied "What job would that be?"

"The one I'm offering you. Working for Sharper Security. I've got a protection detail to start, but you show me you can handle it better than you handle your liquor and I'll train you for patrol and investigation duties. I can already tell by your training and duty record you can handle the physical side of the job. Need to know you can handle the brains and judgment side as well."

Hmmm... might beat staying in prison after all. Short term inmates would run out of money eventually and a reputation for winning would spread among the long term rockheads. Time to demonstrate some of those brains and judgment this guy was looking for, "As long as I don't have to cut my hair again, I'm in. Do I get a uniform to replace this orange jumpsuit? When do I start?"

Sam smiled and gestured towards his very casual outfit, "Surely it's clear I'm not a big stickler for dress codes? But I'll get you a uniform, and then you start right away, if you're willing. I want to take you to meet the lady you'll be protecting. Heck, I still need to meet her myself."

Sam stood, gestured John to follow, and then walked out the office door. He led John down the hallway to a solid steel door with the word "Armory" on it. Hearing the door unlock in response to an unseen command, Sam led John through the doorway and into a large room filled with metal cage lockers and military equipment.

John looked around at all the toys evident in the room. Pistols, shotguns, rifles, crew-served weapons firing projectiles and launching various types of grenades. Riot armor, desert pattern camouflage combat suits of body armor with a small Sharper Security logo. Private sovereign security must pay well.

The variety of equipment astonished John. There were multiple types of shotguns, a relatively rare weapon in his experience, including door breachers, short-barrel automatics with a drum clip designed for close combat, and rapidly firing street sweepers with bulbous ammunition stores.

Sam noticed John's interest in the shotguns, "The shotguns fire fragmentation or high explosive grenade rounds as well. Very effective for the intimidation factor." John thought he'd certainly be intimidated by the air filled with rapid-fire grenades.

Turning around to look at everything else, John caught sight of the most impressive pieces of equipment, a trio of black stealth powered warrior suits. With armor from the Institute for Soldier Nanotechnologies at MIT, the suits were soft and pliable in normal use, but became rigid protection when struck by a projectile. Their muscle-augmenting capabilities were further enhanced by a lower-body exoskeleton. John couldn't wait to be allowed to give one of them a try.

Sam pulled out an electronic key and opened a wall locker with "John Parkur" labeled above it, which happened to have a Sharper Security uniform John's size, complete with utility belt containing hand cuffs and firearm, plus military-style boots and a thin suit of body armor.

"Apparently this whole job idea didn't come as much of a surprise to you as it did to me." John said sardonically as he picked up an expensive encrypted military radio out of his locker and hefted it. "This is surprisingly light."

"But effective. Long range and spread spectrum." Sam handed John the locker's electronic key, "Stick around and maybe you'll learn something, but just when you think you have it all figured out is usually a good time to look for what you're missing. That's lesson number one."

Porter Road, Maricopa, Arizona Zone

That afternoon

Evie slowly awoke. She felt the bed beneath her before opening her eyes and remembering the hospital. The doctor had been in earlier and announced that while she needed some rest and painkillers, they'd let her out within a day or two. Her left side was still on fire, but only at a dull roar beneath the painkillers. Her pulse felt like it was racing to catch-up.

Her room was small, but private. Her bed, a few medical machines, a video screen and camera on the wall, and a couple of padded chairs for visitors. Seemed fairly pleasant to her, especially the video screen and the bed adjustments. She had a button to summon a nurse to the video screen and a slider to indicate her pain level for the machinery to take into account with her medication dosing. The telepresence robot came in and checked on her periodically. Likely cheaper than paying a trained human to walk between rooms.

At a knock on the door, she called out "Come in." Two men entered, both in similar khaki uniform shirts. One wore denim short pants and imported running shoes, the other wore pants to match his shirt and military-style work boots. The firearms and handcuffs hanging from their utility belts spelled law enforcement to Evie. "May I help you?" she said to the older one in short pants.

He glanced around the room as if evaluating it for vulnerabilities, and then stepped over to the side of the bed and extended his hand, "Sam Harper, Sharper Security. Evie, I presume?"

Evie nodded and shook his hand delicately, "Pleased to meet ya." Good solid grip.

Sam smiled, "You too. This is John Parkur, one of my employees." He gestured toward the muscular dusty-faced man with a black ponytail accompanying him into the room.

"Afternoon, Ma'am." John said as he nodded. She could almost see the tip of a non-existent hat in his movement. She recognized the light body amour John wore. John seemed more intense than his more laid-back and casual companion.

She watched briefly as John also surveyed the room, and then nodded back to him, "So pleased."

"How are you feeling?" Sam inquired.

"Better than yesterday." In fact, the pain in her side had diminished even more. No more pain, but now her skin felt a little clammy.

"I understand you had quite an experience at your home yesterday. My people said they found you unconscious in the back yard. I hope you've been treated well and are satisfied with the service."

She nodded, "Quite satisfied with the service. Absolutely devastated at the damage, especially my personal belongings. Really quite stressful, you know." She wasn't going to cry, but it was a little hard to breathe when she talked about the damage to her home, to Hamish's things.

Sam continued, "As you should be aware, Sharper Security will be investigating exactly what happened and pursuing the perpetrators to bring them to justice."

Evie felt her pulse slow down, "I know I signed a contract for security with you when I purchased the home, but that was only a few days past. I'm not really clear on how things work here in Arizona Zone after the Big Split. Isn't there a government agency or something that handles these sorts of matters? I'm afraid I rushed a bit into emigrating here. Seemed like such a good idea at the time. Now I'm not so sure." This conversation is important, she thought to herself. Stay pleasant. Don't be overwhelmed. Need to focus.

"Oh, I think you'll grow to like it here. Having your house destroyed just as you are moving in is a fairly unusual occurrence. Typically it takes weeks for something like that to happen to our new residents."

"I'm glad you can joke about my loss. It seems a bit more serious to me." She tried to sit up a little more primly and put on her business face, but her clammy skin defeated her.

Sam seemed to realize he'd gone a bit far and tried to make amends, "I have some questions for you, and I'll explain how things work around here, but first, I'd like to assure you that we take your safety very seriously. John here has been assigned as your personal bodyguard until we get to the bottom of things. He's very experienced, a former U.S. Marine. Even spent some time on an ambassador's protection detail in Africa before the Big Split put an end to funding for public standing armies."

John added, "I'll be responsible for your safety, Ma'am."

"Evie. You can just call me Evie, John." It was definitely becoming hard to focus. She reached over and adjusted the pain threshold slider on the machine down a bit to report a lower pain level in order to give herself some more clarity.

"Thank you Ma'am. I'll just look around a bit." John proceeded to look over the room some more, paying special attention to the window and the electronics.

Sam continued as John reviewed the area, "Coming from Britain, if you didn't research it much before your trip, you may not be aware how much legal matters here have diverged. We still share a basis in common law, but in the Arizona Zone specifically, we don't share sovereignty. Each landowner, or anyone else who wants police or military protection, contracts with a private sovereign security company for protection. What protection they can expect depends on the details of their contract, although several standard contracts have evolved. The sovereign security company, in our case, Sharper Security, insures against crime and property damage. Theoretically, we could just pay you the specified contractual liquidated damages for what you've gone through, but we find it's better for both of us to provide justice in the form of investigating and holding responsible the individuals who do the damage. Cheaper for us to take it out of their hide and more satisfying for you to get your payment from them."

Hmmm.... "So what assurance do I have that you will keep your side of the contract?" Evie knew quite well from her constable training that Britain had a common law background as well, but it was interesting to see how things worked here in comparison. She could feel herself starting to focus better as she put her current circumstances behind her.

Sam seemed affronted, "First, our reputation depends on it. If we started cheating or abusing our customers, we'd quickly run out of customers. It's more profitable to collect a monthly or annual fee than it is to rob someone once and then be out of business. Second, all you'd have to do is cancel our contract and sign up with a competitor, then ask the competitor to enforce your rights against us. Or even sell your claim against us to someone with the power to enforce it. At that point, we'd have to either make things right or go to war, which isn't exactly profitable either, not to mention a bit physically risky."

"And if someone's not around to collect on their debt from someone who killed them?" Evie asked. Seems like an issue of practicality. Hard to collect on your rights if you're dead.

"Then either their relative collects, sells the debt, or maybe a friend takes care of it. You kill someone's family and you'll find it pretty hard to pay someone to protect you from justice. We still have morals, you know. Without a strong sense of justice, you don't last in this business. Or at least, you don't prosper and neither do your members. I could tell you some stories, but we don't have all day..."

Evie thought she'd found the flaw in the system, "That makes sense, but why doesn't someone with an arms factory set themselves up as a dictator? Or a group of your companies get together and do it?"

"It's been tried... but not very successfully. We're an independent bunch out here and we like it that way. Sure, theoretically you could get enough people with weapons together to try and take over, but realize that there are thousands of sovereign security companies in the Arizona Zone and the one thing we've all agreed to in our mutual contracts is to get together against anyone who looks like they're trying to run roughshod over everyone else. Not only that, but people like to know that the company they contract with can really handle itself without having to be the absolute biggest around. That means underwriting, just like any other kind of insurance. There are big defense companies that don't do anything but live nice, train, and stand ready to back up the littler guys. Medieval Iceland had something similar for a few hundred years. It ended when the Catholic Church started taxing people no matter who they signed up with, but we've modernized the system quite effectively."

Making a mental note to look up medieval Iceland sometime, Evie asked "So what happens if my neighbor shows up with a tank and says to put up or shut up?"

"Someone comes at Sharper Security with a big enough army we can't handle it, and I can have a division of tanks on the roads and a force of attack helicopters overhead from my underwriters within the an hour. Sure, it happens too often and they'll raise our rates, which I'd have to pass on to my customers or go out of business, but just the knowledge they're out there and ready is generally enough to keep anyone from buying expensive hardware in order to see it burn. People are generally smart enough to realize that it's a death sentence to go up against a sovereign security company secure in their contracts with their underwriters. Now, if someone breaks their contracts and can't be trusted, no one's going to back them up when the going gets tough, but we all seem to find that peace suits us quite well. At least. Those of us still alive and in business cooperate just fine."

"Why don't the underwriters take over? Sounds like they've got all the force and you'd struggle to stop them." Her pulse started racing again as she struggled with the pain in her side.

Sam smiled, "Remember, the members of the underwriting companies don't necessarily want to risk their own lives for nothing. If one of the big defense companies went crazy for some reason and their own people didn't restrain them, the little guys are plenty big enough to gang up on them, let along the dozen other big defense companies. Any one of them can credibly protect itself by threatening to nuke any attacker if they're defeated and have nothing else to lose, but the same threat doesn't work during an attack against someone else with a tactical nuke. No, there's an occasional subtle Special Forces style conflict, but it isn't in anyone's interest to be seen as starting a war. Other companies tend to gang up on whoever is disturbing the peace. Bad for business. We want people to feel safe, happy and protected, and I fancy we're better at it than the people who used to run things over here."

Evie shook her head, "Still seems strange to me. So you're my what, head of government?" Doesn't look like much, to be a head of government in short pants.

"No, just the guy whose job it is to protect you. You pay us and we take care of you. Simple commercial transaction where we all do what we do best and all benefit as a result. I'm no good at cooking anything outside a microwave, but I eat well anyway because I pay someone who is. It's all the same; my specialty is just stopping crime and violence. Despite my joke earlier, things are generally pretty quiet for Sharper Security subscribers. We're well respected, so our members are generally left alone, except for personal grudges and the occasional idiot from someplace like La Raza Council. Even those are fairly rare. We have a better crime rate than Britain, where you came from, especially places like London where law and order have essentially broken down."

"Fascinating. You protect mostly individuals?" Law enforcement certainly works differently here. She could see how it might be better, although the pain in her side and the memory of her new home begged to differ. At least the clamminess in her skin was gone.

"Mostly. I have some commercial contracts, but I specialize in individuals and families. Sometimes extended families, like the Barros. Speaking of good cooks, they make great pizza and subs in town. I also run a nicer prison, as prisons go, and do some subcontracting to other companies. There are others that specialize in mostly commercial work, but I'd rather work with the people I contract with directly to solve problems than patrol malls and hotels for drunks."

Evie guessed that people wouldn't pay for a service they didn't at least believe was valuable. "I noticed your signs around the neighborhood. Group discount?" The pain in her side dulled and the clamminess returned. She glanced over and saw that the pain monitor was back to the high setting all of a sudden. Had she adjusted that again?

"Yeah, I make neighborhoods a good deal. If I can get the vast majority of homes for coverage, I can sell it cheaper because I don't have to cover much ground. It's a lot less expensive to provide coverage for three or thirty houses right next to each other than it is if they're scattered across the city. Everybody wins... well, except for my competitors."

Well nobody was being forced to pay. She'd have to think about this. Wasn't exactly what she was used to and she was feeling a bit shabby and played out, "Can we continue this a little later. I'm still a might tuckered."

"Sure. John'll be right outside your door and I'll leave you my personal contact number. I'd like to have a look at your house. I'll come back in a few hours, after you've had a chance to rest, and we can discuss what happened."

"Thank you." Evie said as he made his way to the door. Her muscles felt limp. Time to take a nap.

John just said "Ma'am" and took up his post outside.

Sam handed John a small device to lock the door shut by sliding it under the door and clamping the door itself to the door frame at the bottom. "Protect Evie."

"Aye, Aye, Sir."

He was lucky. His device in room C3 was on the same local network as her room. Probably all the rooms on the floor were connected to one place. At least all the medical devices. The cameras and other security stuff appeared to be on another network. Looking at the welcome message when tried to login to the control port of the combination switch/router the devices all connected to, the operating system running it was at least a year out of date. They must not update it regularly, even though it had to be policy, even at an old hospital like this one. Someone wasn't doing their job.

With judicious use of a known security hole he found online and a little information spoofing, he logged into and took control of the router. Now he controlled all the network communications on the floor. He continued snooping around the hospital network, using Wireshark to view the packets of information as they flowed between the devices in her room.

After watching the communication from the pain threshold indicator to the expert system controlling the drug dosage machine, he experimented with copying the payloads of earlier network packets he'd seen to see if he could convince the expert system to accept information he supplied as valid. He could see the confirmations go back, so it appeared he was able to simulate the conversation.

He started looking closer at the big router he controlled, thinking about ways to interrupt communications without setting off enough alarms that someone would feel the need to send a person to physically investigate. Maybe if he recorded and analyzed the normal network traffic from her room to the outside automated monitoring systems, then he could write a packet filter program that changed the information on the fly, or at least close enough to real time to be dismissed as a slight network congestion delay?

Sand Tank Mountains, Sonoran Desert

About that same time

Sergeant Pedro Guerrera of Policía La Raza unstrapped his assault helmet and wiped sweat from his brow. Headquarters might notice if he actually took the thing off, although he was convinced it was safe out here in the middle of nowhere. At worst, they'd startle a desert ram or some quail, neither of which carried weapons deadly enough to require protection from full body armor and associated headgear.

Sometimes all the rules and regulations they had to follow got to him, but he put up with it to make sure his family stayed out of the mierda he'd grown up in.

The desert hike following an old smugglers route through the Tohono O'odham Nation and across the old Goldwater bomb range had been bad enough, but worse than the opportunity to encounter unexploded munitions buried in the desert like land mines was the task ahead, crossing I-8 without detection. Even 40 klicks southwest of Maricopa, he knew there would be sensors along the freeway.

With two fingers extended, Pedro gestured a couple of his assault team members out of the Sand Tank mountains and into motion on diverging courses, scouting ahead and slightly to the side of the nine others in his team. When the two scouts had what he judged as sufficient distance, he led the team in straggling after them. Five more klicks and they'd reach the ribbons of concrete that indicated where they'd cease to be respected members of the community and change clothing into well-armed banditos, possibly to be shot on sight.

The plan was to use a conveniently dry river bed to pass underneath I-8, disabling any sensors they found, and then follow that same river bed north-west until it ended at a ridgeline south-west of the Sharper Security Prison. Pedro hoped Shortee Tejada would be grateful for his team's sweat and likely blood. Their jog-walk-rest-repeat hike should only take another eight hours or so until they reached the ridgeline. Assuming they made it that far.

El Teniente Garcia should come on one of these little hikes sometime, instead of watching comfortably on video at headquarters. A good diet plan of sweating off the fat would do wonders for his physique. Too bad he couldn't arrange a diversion that would let them drive north in assault vehicles, instead of hiking in across the searing desert. Garcia might have even come along on *that* ride.

Cartegna Lane, Maricopa, Arizona Zone

Early Evening

Sam parked his Corvette up the road from the wrecked house and got out to look around. A lone, full trash bin looked out of place near Evie's property.

Broken and smashed autocabs supported what was left of the structure. They'd obviously been traveling fast at impact. He could see tire tracks across the yard. Some of the early autocabs used the driveway, but the later ones obviously curved around the previous wrecks to arrive from different directions. Judging by the amount of dirt and gravel displaced by the autocabs turning in the yard, they must've used the length of the street to get up to speed.

He supposed it could've been an accident, some defect in programming making them all decide to pick-up their next passenger in the middle of Evie's garage, but that didn't seem extremely likely. Looking at the angles of impact, they appeared to have been directed to try and do the most damage to the house. If they were all following the exact same preprogrammed route, the front of each car would have impacted the rear of the car ahead of it. Even if they were all mistakenly directed to different places within the house, they should have used the same angle from the street, but it looked like many of them purposefully avoided the already crashed vehicles, making wide curves in the yard.

With the on-board expert system's safety programming, Sam could possibly explain why the autocabs avoided crashing into other autocabs in the driveway, but that seemed like pretty selective collision avoidance when those same autocabs rammed a house and the autocabs already under the house. No, someone obviously tampered with them. Probably directly controlling at least some of them.

There wasn't any damage to any of the neighboring properties and a couple of dozen autocabs took up a lot of space, even as crushed as they'd become. Whoever tampered with them was targeting this specific house for some reason.

Sam's expert systems, computer programs with a specific purpose and rules to guide them in how to go about their job, had provided him with background information on Evie, whatever was publicly available online, or available from any of the info databases Sharper Security subscribed to.

He started reviewing Evie's background information again in his glasses as he picked his way through the rubble. Former UK law enforcement, retired on half pay a little early, after only 20 years. Widowed, no disability. Maybe made some enemies in her professional life? Perhaps someone waiting for her to retire, so as not to bring the attention and investigation the death of a special constable would bring in London? Had she moved to Arizona Zone thinking she could run away from someone? Hmmm... something to ask her about.

Not much to be found in the rubble. He'd have his crime scene robots come out and process the place, packing anything away that looked like it may be evidence, but it seemed mostly like household items, a broken house and wrecked autocabs. Odd that there were male items mingled among the debris in the garage. She'd apparently brought her dead husband's things with her halfway across the world. Some people were just packrats, he supposed, unable to let things go.

Sam saw a couple of neighbors peeking out from behind curtains. Maybe one of them had seen something useful. He'd need to detail someone to do interviews.

Maybe if he pulled the onboard systems out of the autocabs they wouldn't all be too damaged to provide useful information. He'd seen storage devices survive worse.

The Sharper Security expert systems also supplied Sam with a crime scene package containing video from the rapid response teams, plus anywhere the autocabs involved showed up recently in his local street or home surveillance systems. They didn't capture anything other than autocabs mysteriously deciding to head towards this street for a pickup, but he knew Pierre had drones in the air that night. Maybe one of them overflew the area and caught something. This neighborhood wasn't too far from his subcontract for the land rockets on I-11. Worth checking into.

Sam slid into his Corvette's front seat and started the engine. Pulling away from the house on manual, he called Pierre and put the video on the vehicle's Heads-Up-Display. Usually, Agence de Sécurité was more than willing to cooperate in matters like these, although their last conversation about John hadn't been totally pleasant.

"Evening, Pierre." Sam started out with a pleasant smile, looking for a favor.

Pierre appeared in the video, still wearing his uniform, the office of Agence de Sécurité in the background, "Bonsoir. More bad news, I suppose."

"No news, just wondering if you are able to assist with some information."

"Ah bon." *I see.* "Unfortunately, I have some bad news for you. I've discovered that several Agence sensors on I-8 stopped providing data two hours ago. All at the same time, all in the same area, near where a dry river bed crosses under the freeway."

Sam could see where he was going, "Banditos again? Any further sign of them?"

"These are good. Likely professional. Elite. No sign of them anywhere near the border. No indication of how many in their group."

"Probably on foot. No easy way to hide vehicle tracks. Any aerial surveillance in the area?" Suspecting the answer, Sam needed to pull Pierre back to his information request anyway.

Pierre looked distracted, considering. "None. I have been relying on the ground sensors in the unpopulated areas, while using my ground patrols near high-value immediate response targets and covering up north with aerial drones."

Sam made the turn onto Honeycutt Road and set the autodrive to take him to Flag Health Center, "I'll notify my people and expert systems to keep a closer eye on the area southwest of town. Speaking of aerial drones, did you happen to have a drone covering Cartegna Lane yesterday evening?" Sam transmitted the exact time and location of the attack to Pierre, "One of my subscribers had an unusual attack on her home last night."

"Un moment." Pierre appeared to check his computer for a moment, then responded further, "I did have a drone right over that area just before the time you gave me, but", Pierre's eyes widened, "shortly afterward it was diverted for an emergency, run over by a land rocket and destroyed." Pierre lifted an eyebrow.

Sam believed he knew the land rocket and aerial drone in question, "Any chance it had a live video feed recording saved at your offices before it was diverted?"

Pierre checked some more, paused, and then checked again. "Pardon, Sam, it appears to have been feeding video, but for some reason I can't find a recording. Everything from the drones is supposed to be recorded at all times for later review, but something seems to have happened to the recording."

"Perhaps a glitch related to its destruction caused the recording to terminate abruptly and not get saved in your system." Seemed odd, though. Should be setup for more fault tolerance than that.

"I can ask my son Edmond. I have almost twenty years on him, but he still knows more about these technical matters than I do."

Sam's Corvette turned left onto Porter Road, driving itself toward the Flag Health Center parking lot, "Thank you. Let me know if you find anything. There was a lot of property destruction and my client was almost killed. It may be difficult to get an autocab in Maricopa for a few days as a result."

"Ah, autocabs, I heard of that incident. Very strange. Bonne Chance."

"Good night."

Porter Road, Maricopa, Arizona Zone

About that same time

He stared at the numbers on the screen in his glasses, lying on his back in bed. There, his network packet filter program had isolated the way the medical dosage machine in her room communicated. Now instead of just disrupting it, he could control it; make it do whatever he liked.

Hmmm.... Perhaps she should just suffer for a while? He reduced the flow of her pain medication, convincing the dosage machine she had no pain, while his program automatically and continuously modified the monitoring information it reported to show any remote watchers that everything was just as expected.

He started browsing the catalog of drugs stored in the machine, and then the wider catalog of drugs available for robot delivery to the machine from the hospital pharmacy, looking them up online to see what their effects were, trying to decide his next move. Lasix, a diuretic, Neurontin for seizures, Compazine for nausea, insulin, barbiturates for sedation, Methotrexate? Some interesting possibilities.

John "Wild Horse" Parkur cracked open the door to Evie's hospital room and glanced in for the millionth time, then checked a clock. He'd been watching her and the hospital for four hours. During that time, he'd seen bots come and go with drug reloads for the machine, cleaning bots sanitizing everything, even a bot hanging from the roof to wash the outside of the window, but no people to visit her, unless you counted the nurse on the video screen.

Time to take his fourth trip around the area, scout for any threats. John locked Evie's room behind him with the lock Sam had supplied. If any medical robots wanted in while he was checking the hospital, they'd have to wait in the passageway. He just hoped there wasn't a medical emergency in the ten minutes he'd be gone. Based on her reported condition, he doubted any risk of that, but just in case he was electronically tied into her medical monitors through the magic of technology combined with Sharper Security's good relationship with the hospital. He'd get a copy of any emergency alerts.

John walked down the corridor, dodging around medical robots that carefully avoided him in turn. He suppressed the urge to shout "Gangway!" at them.

He tried to memorize the faces of the visible patients, visitors and staff, looking for anyone out of place. Anyone without an obvious reason to be there, anyone without an obvious purpose, was suspect. He passed the maternity ward. Lots more people there.

He'd guarded ambassadors, but somehow he felt more responsible for Evie's health. On Marine guard detail, he was just one of many involved in embassy security, or on one of the rarer personal protection details, he was still part of a team, following orders. Now he felt exposed, given responsibility for someone obviously in danger, someone who, despite her law enforcement background, appeared weaker.

John stepped into a stairwell, tried to decide if he should check the roof or the other floors first.

He didn't know the likely threat vectors. Didn't know who had it in for her. Didn't know much about his new boss, other than what he'd heard on the Rez about Sharper Security. Always tinted with a dislike of the white people who'd stolen their land and were now neighbors. There was a lot he didn't know, too much.

Deciding to check overhead, John starting rapidly climbing stairs up toward the roof, two at a time. A lot of ground to cover, not enough minutes to cover it in without leaving the room too exposed. On his way back, he'd hit the head on the level Evie resided on.

John also wasn't used to being so far out on a limb. Sure, he'd led details in the marines, small squads of men, but always with clear orders, clearly defined actions and objectives.

He reached the roof and did a 360 of the building perimeter from his vantage point above. "Protect Evie" Sam had said. Clear enough in objective, not as clear in execution. Executing vague orders was supposed to be officer territory. He wasn't in the Marines anymore. Time to start figuring out more on his own. Use his initiative, and whatever other clichés he could think of to boost his morale.

John took the elevator to the ground floor, preferring to not use the same path down as up and wanting to cover more ground. He checked outside the hospital entrance, glancing over the parking lot and rapidly cataloging the cars present. He tried to also start cataloging the attack vectors on Evie's room, evaluating each possible threat for likelihood and for what he could do about it.

Stepping back into the stairwell, he climbed to Evie's floor, past the maternity ward and back into the corridor outside her room. He unlocked the door, glanced in to make sure everything was all right, and then realized uncomfortably he'd forgotten his trip to the head.

Evie started feeling an ache in her side again, waking up to see John peer seriously into the room, and then take his post back up outside the door. She lay back for a few minutes, considering her new life of adventure and trying to relax instead of becoming hysterical.

The ache in her side turned into a sharp pain. She leaned forward a little and moved the slider on the pain meter, asking for more drugs. Shouldn't take more than a few moments and her pain would be washed away again.

From the hallway outside, she could hear John talking to someone, "… all secure. Nothing unusual to report."

Sam's voice responded, "Good work. Take a break."

She heard footsteps as John left rapidly, "I'll hit the head."

Sam pushed the door open and smiled when he saw she was awake, skipping the pleasantries, "I've been out to see your house. Quite a lot of property damage. Do you want it rebuilt just as it was, or do you want to get something a bit more modern?"

"I don't remember much from the ambulance, but I do remember a bit of a mess." She pressed on her side. "Who's going to rebuild it?" she asked suspiciously.

"Sharper Security, of course. Well, not personally, but your property *is* insured enough to pay for a nice rebuild by modern professional contractors. Of course, we'll take it out of whoever did this to you, once we find them. And naturally, we'll be paying your medical bills and any temporary accommodations necessary, from the same source, of course."

She wasn't homeless after all. What a nice thought. "Of course. Why modern style, I suppose. Hadn't thought of it. Never built a house for myself, but I'm sure I'm not going to want the same layout as before. Oh, it was nice enough, even if it is a bit shabby now, but I think I could do without the memories. Really quite stressful."

"You'll get more house in the modern style. Those old stick houses took a lot of labor to put up. Really expensive to recreate, now. With today's automation, you can buy a lot of upgrades with the difference in what you'd have to spend on labor to build something just like you lost. Otherwise, it'd be cheaper to make your new house something already built on another property, but I'd prefer to see you restored on your own property instead. Shows the neighbors that we'll take care of them if necessary, instead of leaving a hole in the block."

She'd be delighted about it if her side didn't hurt so badly and she hadn't just experienced her old, new, home's destruction, "A new, modern home sounds lovely."

Sam changed topics, "I dislike having to bring this up while you are still in the hospital, but it appears the attack on your home was intentional, not accidental." She gasped a little from the pain as he kept talking, "It's apparent the autocabs were tampered with and the scene makes plain they were targeted at your home specifically. Do you have any idea who might want to hurt you?"

She tried to concentrate on his questions, but the pain was beginning to overwhelm her. She stabbed at the pain meter again, pushing the slider against its stopping point.

When she still didn't respond right away, Sam began to look concerned, "Is that thing working right?"

She shook her head, and then gave out a low moan. Her whole body ached, now, with the pain in her side piercing her brain as well.

She could hear John's footsteps arrive back outside the door.

Sam pushed the medical call button for her, while raising his voice just loud enough to be heard outside, "John!"

John pushed his way into the room as she moaned again. No nurse appeared on the video screen

Sam stabbed the button again, "There's something wrong. She's in too much pain. Either she's having a relapse, or the pain medication isn't working."

It definitely hurt. She could feel herself on the edge of passing out from the pain.

John looked at the machine, showed Sam the position of the pain slider at maximum. "Wasn't there last time I checked on her. Maybe the machine's out of pain meds and not talking to their monitoring center anymore to get a refill?"

"Something's wrong. There should be all sorts of alarms going off. Stay here and do what you can for her. I'm going to see if I can find a real person around here." Sam headed out the door.

She felt her pulse pushing blood through her arteries. The pain in her side spread to her chest. She felt like she was suffocating, taking quick short gasps, trying to overcome the pain. The muscles on her left side began to spasm.

He continued blocking the alarms from the monitoring machines and the call button in her room. They showed her pulse racing. She was probably convulsing in pain by now.

He pictured her alone in her room, writhing in pain, unable to contact anyone, unable to get any help. Time to trigger the special delivery he'd arranged as the next step.

John watched Evie squirm in pain, holding the hand cloth he'd doused in cold water from the room's sink against her forehead, hoping Sam came back with help soon. He listened to her moan, rapidly becoming more and more incoherent.

The door pushed open and John expected to see Sam returning with someone, but was disappointed. Just a delivery robot.

Wait, maybe it was arriving with more pain medication. Sure enough, it proceeded to the dosage machine and began loading vials into the back, just as he'd seen another machine do earlier. John hoped it would hurry and finish so the new medicine could reach her blood stream and relieve her pain.

John wondered how long the machine could go without a refill. Obviously not very long, he'd seen the same machine refilled an hour ago. Before that, he'd stood guard at least three hours without seeing it refilled. It didn't make sense to design a system where you had to send a pain refill every hour or put the patient at risk. He dropped the damp cloth on the bed. Like Sam said, something was wrong.

Acting on a hunch and hoping he was right, John pushed the bot roughly away from the dosage machine, and then removed the vials it'd just placed in the back and closed the machine up again. He glanced at the vials, but didn't recognize any of the chemical names. They weren't morphine, the painkiller she was supposed to be on, so he wasn't keeping her from relief.

The bot angrily headed for the door as it opened. Sam and a large male nurse dressed in blue scrubs and carrying a needle and ampoule of morphine rushed in, dodging around the bot.

The male nurse looked at Evie contracting on the bed and holding her side while sweating, and then looked at the pain level slider, "You're right. It's on max, but she's obviously still in pain." He disconnected the dosage machine's connection to her IV drip and replaced it with an injection of morphine, and then pushed the call button, to no avail. "I'm a nurse midwife, not a technician. Must be a malfunction, although I don't know why there aren't alarms going off all over the place and why the call button isn't working. I'll have to get someone from the IT department."

Evie sighed in relief as the pain medication began to take effect. That was close. Her pain appeared to rapidly diminish.

John looked at Sam, who seemed deep in thought. John interrupted whatever Sam was thinking about, showing him the vials, "That bot leaving when you came in was loading these into the drug dosage machine, but another one refilled it only an hour ago. Seemed suspicious to me, so I stopped it."

Evie started to take an interest in the discussion around her. The male nurse looked at the vials in John's hand, "That's certainly not pain medication. I don't even recognize a couple of those, but I'm usually in the maternity ward."

John watched as Sam listened to the male nurse, looked over at Evie to see how she was doing, and then turned back to face John. "Start packing her things."

Happy to have a clear task for a change, John dumped a pillow from its case and started gathering Evie's meager possessions from around the room to fill it with.

Meanwhile, the nurse opened the back of the machine and confirmed it still had plenty of morphine, "Should be another day before actually needing a refill."

"Good job." Sam said to John, for the second time that day. Sam turned to the nurse and smiled, "What do we need to get her out of here immediately? Paperwork?"

Evie seemed to start catching up on what was going on around her, listening in on the conversation. "Was this another attack?" she asked John.

John nodded in response, "Yes, Ma'am."

Evie shook her head. She seemed on the verge of tears, "Really quite stressful."

The nurse pressed the call button again. After he still received no response, the nurse replied to Sam, "Wait here. I need to go call the hospital administration and see what they want me to do about all this."

Sam stepped between the nurse and the door. John could see Sam's eyes flash like pistol muzzles as he stared down the nurse, "We're leaving now. We're taking the patient with us before that dose of morphine you gave her wears off. It may help minimize the damages the hospital is going to pay for this malpractice fiasco if you assist us in every way possible. You can clean up the rest of this mess and figure out what happened later. I'm sure there'll be a full investigation. Actually, I'm surprised hospital security isn't here already. I suggest you preserve the evidence, but again, we aren't waiting."

The male nurse seemed taken aback, "I'll, ah, I'll get her a wheelchair, but there *is* paperwork." John realized he'd only seen Sam pretend to argue with him before. John was pretty sure if someone tried to actually stop them from leaving, Sam would give them a warning before shooting them, but only pretty sure.

Sam relaxed a touch. "Wonderful. We can do the paperwork on the way to the car." he responded. Noticing John standing around with Evie's small collection of things already bagged, Sam added "John, I suggest you help the man with the wheelchair. You can put those in whatever kind of storage it has. I'll explain to Evie and arrange for an emergency medical team to meet us in the parking lot." Sam stepped out of the way of the nurse.

John took that last comment as an order to make sure the wheelchair came back as quickly as possible and followed the nurse out the door. As he left, he heard Evie asking, "Where are we going?"

Hidden Valley Road, Maricopa, Arizona Zone

Late Evening

Sam drove his Corvette up the winding driveway from Hidden Valley Road. The driveway curved around giant cracked black boulders and desert shrubbery while climbing the ridgeline to his home and the orphanage he'd built next door.

After taking Evie from the hospital in town, he'd called Maria to let her know he'd be late. She hadn't been happy. She was directing the kids in the orphanage putting on *"As You Like It"*. The orphanage was for children who'd lost their parents in war, any war, formally declared or not.

Maria knew that wasn't Sam's favorite Shakespeare play. He'd watch their showing in town, but she also expected him to see every full rehearsal at the orphanage.

"You are the Patron!" she would say, "You must attend rehearsal, tell us what you like, what you don't like." He could hear her voice in his head.

At least it wasn't as time consuming as when she'd decided that because he'd lettered in track and field back in high school, he'd be perfect as the Head Field Judge for her week long track meet for the surrounding community. He managed hardly any other work that week, but the meet ended up with great security.

No, he'd much rather just sit in a chair and watch a play, then provide enough comments on the performance to make her happy.

Sam liked that she took her charge to educate the dozens of kids in the orphanage seriously, but sometimes she forgot that he'd hired her and a staff of others for the job. He had his own responsibilities.

Responsibilities that relying on security at the Flag Health Center had almost caused him to fail. He wouldn't make that mistake again. For now, Evie would stay where he could control her whole environment.

Chapter 4 - Day Four

Highway 85, West of Maricopa, Sonoran Desert

First light of dawn

Hauling only one 53 foot semi-trailer behind his tractor truck, Raoul Dominguez was taking it easy, listening to tejano music and watching the scenery while the truck drove itself. Today, he was only making a local run with multiple stops. After loading in the dark at his home base in the west valley, he planned to drive south to Gila Bend, and then north-east through Maricopa to Mesa, with a few diversions along the way to drop off or pick up cargo.

A big dust devil caught his attention as it crossed the road ahead of him, propelled by the changing morning temperatures. The base of the funnel encompassed the whole road and then some and the top reached high into the sky. He told the truck to slow down a little just in case, but he wasn't really worried. With a load in the semi-trailer pressing down, a little wind wasn't going to cause him a problem. What little visibility the dust devil impaired wouldn't affect the systems steering the truck. Not for the few seconds he'd be passing through the heart of the dust.

Now if he'd been facing a sand storm, and it was currently the season for a big haboob, that would worry him. Virtually no visibility, 50-60 mph winds. Usually cross-winds against his semi-trailer, sand and dust 10,000 feet high and up to 50 miles wide. He'd stop and turn around for that, just hoping to out run it. They were pretty common between Phoenix and Tucson. Something about how collapsing summer thunderstorms blew the dry loose sand up from the open desert caused them to form.

Nothing like that on the horizon ahead of him today, though. Just a relatively harmless giant dust devil. More dangerous looking than actually dangerous.

Raoul directly supervised the loading this morning, so he knew everything would be loaded in the order of his planned stops. The more expensive, less used, local roads required for today's deliveries added to his profit. Sure, he paid more per mile, but he also charged his customers more for the added delivery expense. He saved part of that expense by combining multiple deliveries in the same local area as efficiently as possible, increasing his profits.

His biggest delivery today was a glider cockpit destined for the Estrella Sailport. He'd have to work a little with the portable forklift attached to the back of the semi-trailer to get his scheduled pickups loaded around it, but he still thought he'd be home in the west valley by just after dark, even if he stopped for dinner at Barro's Entertainment Metroplex. His media naranja would be expecting him no later than midnight.

Rita Road, South Tucson, La Raza Council

About that same time

Lieutenant Garcia of Policía La Raza swiped his arm angrily across the display table. The touch screen planning table showed a satellite view of the area around Hidden Valley and Farrell Roads. One circle drawn on the table surrounded the Sharper Security Prison, located on the top of a small hill just north-west of the road intersection, latitude 33.036851, longitude -112.155454. A dozen smaller soldier shaped icons, each marked with a latitude and longitude, littered the long black rock ridgeline to the south-west, overlooking the desert valley.

Garcia drew another possible assault route for the team on the ridgeline to follow in approaching the prison, using a local water tower and some homes for partway concealment. In response, the planning table's expert system estimated a 15% chance at least one of the Policía La Raza soldiers would manage to reach the prison alive. That pitiful figure represented a little progress over his last attempt. Frustrated, Garcia swiped the route from the table display again.

Too much open space and too many guarded homes between the broken rock ridgeline and the prison. They had to cross at least 2000 feet from the edge of the ridgeline to reach even the base of the hill the prison occupied. He gestured to tilt the satellite view again, hunting for any sort of cover in the area. The ridgeline rose at least three times as high as the hill, but even so, the hill commanded the immediately surrounding area.

Although the expert system was estimating probabilities of being observed and attacked successfully from the prison for each approach, it wasn't taking into account the idea that Sam Harper had sown the surrounding area with more sensors and hardware. No way to know where those might be located until it was too late, Garcia thought.

Pulling one of the soldier icons marked with "33.031225,-112.168694" on the map towards himself, Garcia opened up a video window from the assault team leader, and then spoke in his ear. "Any sign your position has been compromised?"

Unconsciously glancing at the corner of his helmet where he knew the camera was located, Pedro Guerrera, the assault team leader responded, "Nothing yet. Of course, they could be watching us right now and we'd never know." He peered around the edge of a broken black boulder a little more, "I don't see how we're going to get from here to there without becoming a used piñata."

"Any chance you could pass as one of the locals, maybe just walk up the road to one of the houses nearby as if you belong?" They had to have some way to get there, he'd put a lot on the line just to get them to the ridgeline, hopefully undetected.

Pedro sighed, "El Teniente, even if we weren't carrying enough hardware to knock out the prison's known automated defenses and blow open one of the walls, I'm sure they keep careful track of who belongs in the neighborhood, including identifying visitors to the area. Señor Harper es un muy mal hombre."

"I know", Garcia replied, "without at least an armored vehicle, you're just too exposed crossing the remaining desert. Keep thinking." A priority call flashed on the screen. "I'll call you back."

Answering the call, Garcia was surprised to see el Jefe. "Buenos días." *Good morning.*

"Nothing good about it." El Jefe wore a red silk robe and didn't seem too concerned about his subordinate seeing him next to his bed, nor viewing its current occupants, as beautiful as they were. "Victor Tejada just woke me up to inquire about the welfare of his son."

Garcia got straight to the point, "Shortee Tejada is still in prison, but my men are only half a klick away. We were discussing the best approaches to the prison when you called."

El Jefe pulled aside the top of his robe, exposing his hairy chest. "It wounds me in el corazón to hear that my subordinates have not yet carried out my wishes. That you wait until I am stabbed through the heart by my rivals before you perform this simple task. The image of Policía La Raza is one of power, but you threaten to make it one of impotence. No more delay in this matter."

El Jefe drew a finger across his throat and the connection cut off.

Garcia felt the message was clear enough and summoned Pedro again to the screen, "We have our orders. The rescue must proceed today. No later than this evening, so you can use the night to evade and escape."

Pedro seemed in a better mood for this call, "Your idea about an armored vehicle set me thinking. I can't get one of those in here undetected, but I may have something good enough to get us to the road near the prison."

Hidden Valley Road, Maricopa, Arizona Zone

Later that morning

Evie stretched out in the prison infirmary bed and yawned, taking care not to disturb her IV line. The grey walls and high security weren't pretty, but she felt safe behind thick steel walls with automatic gun turrets. A lot safer than the last couple of days, anyway. She'd seen much more of the Sharper Services EMT taking care of her since last night than she'd seen of any of the hospital staff in her previous stay.

The two handcuffed prisoners in the room next door, separated only by a glass partition, spoiled the mood a bit. She was still absolutely devastated by the attacks against her, but she could feel herself regaining some strength after a night's rest. The pain in her left side was barely noticeable.

John appeared in the doorway and looked in on her. He must've been alerted to her waking up by the prison surveillance system, but he'd obviously also slept nearby. John looked a little rumpled, as if he hadn't slept in a proper bed, just in his uniform clothing somewhere uncomfortable. "How are you feeling?" he asked.

"A bit shabby, but none the worse for wear, considering." She felt shafted and could use some makeup, but somehow she doubted that was something they kept in the Sharper Security prison infirmary as standard supplies.

"I've already sent a message to Sam that you're awake. He'll be here shortly. We've got to figure out who's responsible for these attacks." That was about the longest sentence she'd heard him speak in the time he'd been guarding her.

"Are you a local?" she cautiously asked, not sure how to find out more about him without risking offense.

John smiled and stepped into the room, over to her bedside, "I'm from the local Rez, if that's what you mean. Pima Indian, Akimel O'odham, descended from a long line of Gila River People. The tribe controls more than half a million acres of land."

Apparently, he wasn't adverse to opening up a little, "I'm glad to have you protecting me. I'm gutted and a long way from South Croydon. Don't know what I'd do, otherwise. It's just a struggle."

He nodded, whipping his long black ponytail a little, "I was born and raised on the Rez, but grew up in the United States Marine Corps. Can't get rid of me too easily. I'm responsible for you now."

Evie could hear the capital letters in his speech and decided John was the bee's knees, "Brilliant. Glad we've got that sorted."

John looked a little confused at that but she could tell he fancied her a bit, although he was quite young. She hadn't completely lost it, even lying on a hospital bed with no makeup.

Evie noticed Sam standing inside the doorway. That man walked so quietly he could sneak up on you without even intending to. Today he was in denim short pants again, this time with a tan colored soft cotton polo shirt and running trainers.

"You're quite the nob, for a plod." She commented. He really owned this whole place on top of the hill?

Sam seemed to be consulting some sort of online translation service, "Thank you, I think."

"No worries. I retired as a detective inspector, so was quite the mod plod myself." Evie was quite chuffed about her rank.

"I know enough about Britain to know that your police don't usually retire after only 20 years. Why the early retirement?" Sam had obviously been checking up on her.

"That's a bit personal, isn't it?" Quite cheeky, really.

Sam explained patiently, "With your background, you should understand that I'm trying to catch whoever is responsible. Since they appear to be targeting you in an ongoing campaign, they obviously have some sort of grudge. The more I know about your background that's relevant, the easier it will be for me to put something together and solve this." Of course, she knew that, she just wasn't used to being on this side of the interviewing. Well, not very often.

"If you must know, I retired after my husband Hamish was killed in the Unison Riots. I couldn't stand London, nor the job anymore. My heart wasn't in it." Shame on him, pushing her into that. Now she felt like crying.

"How did he die?" Sam asked. Why did he have to make her revisit it all in her mind?

"Hamish was on the job with the Transport police, leading a few of his men and a larger group of special constables to protect the tube. A street mob caught them outside the tube entrance. The specials panicked. They're only volunteers, after all." She sniffled.

"The tube?" John asked.

"The underground... mass transit. Underground trains. You know?"

"The subway?"

"No, trains, not walkways. Trains going on rails underground." Sometimes Evie thought these people didn't speak English.

Sam pressed on through the interruption, "And then what happened?"

She felt her eyes dimming with the recollection, "I saw the video from the street cameras. I liked to watch Hamish while he was working. I saw it live from headquarters. Hamish told the Unison people to disperse with a loudhailer. The bloody rioters started throwing bricks. The specials ran for the tube. They broke the ranks the regulars had them in, their formation disintegrated. Most of the regulars followed, every man for himself, no longer able to protect each other. The Unison crowd was wearing scarfs and gas masks, wielding baseball bats and crowbars. Hamish wasn't armed. We don't arm the regular constabulary in London. They carry clear shields and batons on riot duty."

John muttered something under his breath, but Evie didn't quite catch it, lost in her story.

"I could tell Hamish knew if they all ran, the mob would overrun them from behind. They're only protected if they stand in line, shield to shield. From behind, they're just men in padded clothing unable to run very fast. He looked up at the camera. Looked right at me, as if he knew I was watching, then grabbed his riot baton and faced the rioters alone."

Evie sniffed and wiped tears with the back of her hand. "Hamish was good. He knocked down almost a dozen before they overwhelmed him. Beat him to death. They focused on him, as if he was their purpose for rioting. Forgot about his men. *They* all got away, reformed right at the tube entrance into a new wall. He gave his men the time. The rioters were all gone when I got there. Good thing. I'd have killed them myself."

Sam nodded and produced a box of tissue from a shelf, "I know this is hard for you. I appreciate you answering our questions. Was there any indication someone was targeting your husband? Someone who may have followed you here to do you damage?"

"I don't know. I don't believe so. The official investigation concluded he was a hero and the rioters were an out of control mob. They never caught anyone. The whole city was one big riot that week. They were lucky to keep it from burning to the ground or poisoning the inhabitants from the tear gas all over the streets."

"I imagine you were part of the investigation, at least informally?" Sam stated more than inquired while she blew her nose.

"Yes, they gave me courtesy copies of everything, but not really my department. Later, after the new civil service contract, they declared an amnesty. Oh, not for murder, but for rioting. That made it hard to pressure anyone to give up who was involved in specific incidents. We could prove they were rioters, but they just yelled amnesty and claimed they didn't know anything about his death. After that, I retired. Half pay isn't much, but it's enough." Her friends hadn't understood. They hadn't seen their husband beaten to death on a London street. How could they expect her to ever ride the tube again?

Sam shook his head. "European justice. Anyone else with a grudge against you? You must have made some enemies in your line of work."

John glared at Sam a little, as if he thought she'd had enough. Rubbish, she was tougher than she looked.

Evie cleared her throat, trying to answer with calmness. "I'm sure there were a few. None stick out to me. None that aren't in prison, or that didn't have plenty of time to come after me in London. I did my job. Kept my nose clean. Moved up the ranks. Made sergeant early. Special promotion."

"Anyone make any threats recently? Not so recently?"

Evie thought for a minute, "No... nothing recently. The Home Office in London might have some old emails with threats in them, but nothing serious. They happened to everyone. We never took them too seriously."

Sam checked his notes, "These attacks seem pretty personal, not random. I'm looking for a revenge motive. This most recent attack. Ever poison anyone, even accidentally? Ever cause anyone great pain? Ever involved in a medical accident to someone? Maybe a family member who wants revenge for pain caused a love one?"

Evie sighed and mopped up the last of her tears. "No. Nothing like that."

"The first attack, on your house, looked like someone really wanted to destroy your home. Even more than actually trying to harm you directly. Ever destroyed anyone's home?"

Evie thought some more, "No ... well, no one still alive. Spent a few fortnights on exchange in France early in my career with a GIGN intervention force. Wasn't really my operation, lots of second-guessing and micromanaging, but I was nominally in charge just after I made Sergeant. We took down a suspected terrorist apartment in Paris. None of the suspected terrorists left alive. Real cock up. I was young, then." Wasn't my fault. Just following orders from above. Not making waves.

"GIGN?" John asked, copying her pronunciation of the acronym.

"Groupe d'Intervention de la Gendarmerie Nationale", she recited, "French special operations. Counter-terrorism, that sort of thing. I worked for MI5 in London, they had an exchange program. That was back when relations were a little closer than they are now. Diplomacy, working together and all that. Very touchy-feely stuff. While I was a patrol constable, I stumbled across a radical Muslim terrorist cell. Went to the wrong apartment looking for a bloke with a warrant. They weren't home, but their pad was full of explosives. Sheer dumb luck, but it got me into detective constable training, put me on the fast track to detective sergeant and marked me out for counter-terror training later."

"No one left alive? No enemies from that? Not even bureaucratic enemies?" Sam pressed.

"There was one fellow it upset. Local GIGN non-commissioned officer who worked for me. He tried to undermine me from the start, always disputing orders from above. Not really a team player. After the deaths, he tried to blame me for it all, but I still protected him. After all, it was really all the terrorists fault, not Pierre's. If the terrorists hadn't used the family as cover, they'd never have been hurt. Just in the wrong place at the wrong time. Dumb luck again, I suppose. Apparently, Pierre had evidence the family was innocent just before GIGN blew the apartment walls in, but I was happy Pierre was cleared. He did what he could." It really wasn't her fault. She never intended for them to kill an innocent family, she was just trying to do her job.

Sam looked thoughtful, "Pierre? Happen to remember his last name?"

Evie thought for another moment, "No... it was a long time ago. About eighteen years. I remember he was cute, in a French way. Long flowing hair, that sort of thing."

Now John looked thoughtful and started to say something, but Sam quieted him with a gesture and started working something on the screen on his glasses, eyes glancing around furiously to give commands to his computer. "Would you recognize Pierre if you saw him again?"

"I suppose. As I said, it's been a long time and he'll be a lot older." She lay back and shuffled around in her bed. This whole thing was really quite stressful.

Sam turned a medical monitor around, "I'm patching some video into this monitor from the main system. Not really intended for lineups, but it'll have to do."

Evie watched as an older man with long silver hair in a blue uniform appeared on the screen, mouthing words. "That could be him. It's hard to say for sure." She knew how unreliable memory could be.

Sam continued looking things up online, "I'm checking his record. He runs Agence de Sécurité in Casa Grande, another sovereign security group in a nearby town. Immigrated here 16 years ago. His background and qualifications on the Agence information site list him as a former non-commissioned officer in Groupe d'Intervention de la Gendarmerie Nationale."

John interjected, "The timing is right. Same name, looks like the same man. Might have seen you come over here, remembered his old grudge now that you were in reach, decided to do something about it."

Sam looked thoughtful again and turned to John, "There was a black Camaro in the parking lot of Agence de Sécurité when we were there the other day. The same car was in the parking lot at the hospital when I dropped you off to start protecting Evie. I think we have our first genuine break in this case." Maybe she wouldn't have to run forever.

"I'm glad my painful memories were some use after all."

Sam looked back at her, "I'll do some more checking on Pierre and get the hospital to release their surveillance footage of that night, see if Pierre belongs with that black Camaro. With what they let happen to you, we've got some leverage. I have to tell you, though; I've worked with Pierre locally for several years. I'm not sure I like him as a back-shooter. He has a good reputation and has always dealt with me straight."

John frowned, "Not with me. Wouldn't be the first good man to turn bad over an old grudge from his past. Maybe he's trying to protect that good reputation."

"Maybe." Sam considered, "But I find it best to reserve judgment on these things until I have all the facts. A couple of things still don't completely fit, but he could just be creating clever alibis. It's not like he doesn't know the business from the other side."

Evie thought Sam was being overly cautious. She'd been part of plenty of investigations and this was too much of a coincidence to be passed off as meaningless. Pierre must be their man.

"Either way", Sam added, "It's going to be a tricky situation. Agence de Sécurité has lots of men and plenty of weapons for those men to use. Pierre is in charge of them all. If he's guilty, we either need to take him by surprise, or by overwhelming force. I doubt he's going to come down and surrender himself at the prison gates. Mishandled, this could start a war. A lot more people could get killed. I need to make some calls."

She was getting tired, anyway. "I believe I'll have a nap."

Sam headed for the door, followed by John. John paused at the doorway, "I'll be just outside. Let me know if you need anything."

She smiled at the proper hero, "I will."

Cowtown Road, Casa Grande, Arizona Zone

That afternoon

Sam turned his black and white Corvette from Cowtown Road into the mostly deserted parking lot of Agence de Sécurité. He didn't see the black Camaro, although he'd already ensured Pierre would be there by having his electronic secretary make an appointment on behalf of someone who wasn't going to show up.

Sam took a moment to check the escape routes, parking close to the tan stone headquarters, pointing his Corvette toward the railroad tracks that paralleled the road. Assuming he made it to his car alive, he anticipated following the tracks would more likely evade any Agence de Sécurité vehicles responding to a call to converge on their headquarters.

After that, the tall desert brush would obscure his vehicle quickly. The gravel base of the tracks spilled over to form a narrowly passable road that wouldn't create a plume of dust like the nearby dirt roads would. Passable as long as a train wasn't coming, but the Corvette's onboard AI could track that for him.

Sam's first choice wouldn't normally be to beard the lion in his lair, but he didn't plan to try and make an arrest today. He preferred to interview Pierre in person, where he'd be most comfortable, feel most protected, and perhaps more willing to tell the truth, or at least let something of it slip through.

He didn't think Pierre would panic enough to try and hold him, even if Pierre *was* guilty. Why start an ultimately losing war before you needed to, especially if you weren't sure what evidence existed against you? Still, Sam made sure he'd stacked the odds of an escape as much in his favor as possible. The "quick" and the "dead" was nice, but "prepared" generally beat "quick", most days.

Sam entered the building, stepping quickly and lightly to the counter, already aware from previous trips that the recessed automated weapons were physically prevented from directly aiming at it. Even with several inches of bullet resistant plate glass, Pierre was smart enough to not want a fusillade of bullets directly towards an employee behind the counter.

Pierre smiled from behind the counter, "Bonjour. This visit is an unexpected pleasure."

"Decided to drop by." Sam responded casually, "Anything new on the video from that destroyed drone?" Sam noted Pierre appeared to be alone, at least in this front lobby area. More Agence officers might be in the back.

Pierre seemed as easy going as usual, no signs of unusual stress or strain, beyond maybe a little lack of sleep from keeping an eye on his border with La Raza. "Unexpectedly, ah, nothing in the system."

Staying casual, Sam added, "The victim is someone you may know. Recently emigrated from Britain. I'm transmitting the file photo with her name to you. Recognize her?"

Sam could see recognition dawn in Pierre's eyes as he reviewed the transmission and gasped "Evie? After all these years? Can it be?" Either Pierre was a great actor, or his surprise was genuine.

"Yes, she says she worked with you in Paris, a long time ago."

Pierre shook his head, "Yes, that is true, many years ago, but I never expected to see her again. Sacre Bleu!"

Sam waited to see what Pierre might add.

The longer Pierre thought about the past, the more negative emotion deepened the lines in his face. "I hope you are not involved with this woman. She is not to be trusted, not in any way. Yes, I worked with her. Rather, for her. That is what cost me my career, drove me to America." Maybe there *was* something here, Sam thought.

"Tell me about her. What happened with you and Evie?"

"I made a fresh start here. My son is the only one who knows all the details of my past in France. I thought I'd left all that behind."

Sam thought that sounded promising, "How did you come to leave France?"

"I was working as part of a DSGE Intervention Force detail. The politicians had some stupid idea of an exchange program that went beyond just training and observation. It's seared in my memory, now. They wanted to 'Enhance the counter-terrorism ability of NATO', through 'cross-cultural exchanges'. What it amounted to was putting officers from each counter-terror service in charge of operations in another country. The idea was that everyone would be forced to learn something about each other. Instead, it was a disaster."

"Evie was the only female counter-terror detective sergeant in MI5 at the time. Supposed to be a hot up and comer, on track for rapid promotion, so they inflicted her on us as ze nominal commander. She was worthless. Preferred to flirt, tour Paris shops, and rely on her compatriots in MI5 to tell her what was happening. She 'led' our team assigned to investigate threats toward several summertime tourist events in Paris."

"We discovered threats, describing planned suicide bomber attacks on the tourist events, but with very specific details. Almost too specific in what was planned. There were a lot of disaffected and radicalized Muslims in France back then. The more radical Mullahs had support among the young Muslims who couldn't find jobs, which was most of them. They wanted someone to blame for their lack of a future."

"How'd you find out about the threats?" Sam asked.

"MI5. A confidential source provided ze details. They traced ze details to an apartment in Paris. Discussed what to do about them. That's when Evie had her brainchild. Suicide bombers might blow themselves and a lot of something else up if you didn't surprise them fast enough, right? Her 'brilliant' plan was to use breaching charges and blow all four walls in at the same time, followed by flash-bang grenades. The terrorists would be disoriented and not know what was happening long enough for DSGE to take them all down safely."

Well, Pierre had the bitter attitude down pat. This wasn't exactly how Evie'd told the story.

"We were fooled by ze terrorists, or by someone else. Time was very short and cooler heads did *not* prevail. The IP address ze threats were traced to was in use by the occupants of the apartment. We watched, monitoring their ISP. We tracked back some attempts to break into ze public transportation computers from their IP, which proved to ze higher ups we were dealing with a serious terrorist cell. Everyone saw what they wanted to see. Just before ze tourist events mentioned in the threats were scheduled to start, ze higher-ups on both side decided to approve Evie's plan."

Sam wondered how much of the story was hindsight talking. He was sure Pierre had gone over this a million times in his mind in the years since. Maybe changed a couple of things in the process. Memory could be a funny thing.

Pierre continued bitterly, "We didn't want to alert ze terrorists, so we stayed away from ze neighbors. Government records showed ze apartment was rented by a young Muslim couple, married ze year before. Evie called it a cover. Coconspirators. Accomplices. She was sure ze real terrorists were using them as a front."

"I pulled the surveillance tapes from the parking garage attached ze building. The car registered to the couple had left ze building with two visible occupants, male and female, in ze front seats, just before the ISP records showed ze attack on the public train system computers. The pictures from the car matched the license pictures of the young couple. The wife didn't wear a hijab. I doubt they were even practicing Muslims, let alone cover for ze terrorists."

"I'd spent all night reviewing the parking garage video, looking for suspects. By the time I figured it out, put ze time frame together, confirmed ze occupants of the vehicle, we had only minutes until ze scheduled explosion. Evie wouldn't listen. She seemed distracted, even though she was ze official commander on the scene. The only one who could postpone things without going to higher authority."

"They botched the breaching explosions. Wouldn't have been so bad, but they targeted a kitchen wall for one of the breaches, thinking no one would be using it early on Saturday morning. Shrapnel from the explosion killed ze wife. The husband was shaving in ze bathroom, another designated entrance point. I imagine she was making him an early breakfast. He too died."

"And the terrorists?" Sam asked.

"There were no explosives in ze apartment. No terror plans, no threats. No connections to radical Islam. Just a computer infected with malware being used as the end of a chain of anonymous proxies hiding ze real source. Nothing."

Sam briefly pictured his own reaction in the same situation. "That must've been upsetting." he under exaggerated, looking for a response.

"Of course, there was an inquiry. Devastated, I told ze truth about what happened. Evie blamed me for not bringing her ze evidence sooner. Said there just wasn't time to stop things, that I hadn't acted fast enough. Spent too much time looking at ze parking garage video. She was whisked back off to England. MI5 protected their own fair-haired child."

"And you?" Sam prodded.

"DSGE officially exonerated me. I brought ze evidence to my superior, as required. Unofficially, my career was over. After being linked to that fiasco, there was no chance for promotion. No challenging assignments. I'm surprised they found me a desk to fill. That's when I decided to emigrate here. For a fresh start."

Sam brought the discussion back around to its original purpose. "It doesn't sound like you'd be happy to see Evie again."

"No.... happy doesn't describe what I am feeling right now, my friend. I wish she'd never entered my life. Please tell me you haven't allowed yourself to be caught up with her."

"She's a client and appears to be a victim of a crime. I'll do what I can for her, but thank you for your frank answers. I'll let you know what happens."

"Bonne Chance."

Sam stopped at the door, leaning back to face Pierre, but ready to depart quickly, "Oh, one more thing. The last time I was here, I noticed a black Camaro. Your car?"

"Yes. Well, Edmond usually drives it. Why?"

"You've seen my Corvette? I appreciate performance classic cars. We'll talk more later, after I have the opportunity to check some things."

Turned out Sam didn't need to use his quick getaway plan. Perhaps next time.

Hidden Valley Road, Maricopa, Arizona Zone

Dusk

Pedro led his men in a careful exfiltration of the ridgeline, backing over the crest in leapfrog fashion, carefully avoiding the driveway and yard of a mansion built on the top of the ridge, and then hiking south-east toward where Hidden Valley Road followed a low pass through the area.

Arriving at the side of the road, Pedro directed all but one of his men to take cover behind giant black broken boulders close to the edge of the road. He took the last man's helmet and body armor, and then replaced his automatic rifle with a Y-shaped walking stick he'd cut for the purpose.

Pedro found his own hiding place nearby and settled in to wait a few minutes.

Raoul cruised up the road, listening to his Tejano music, keeping track of his location on the digital map in front of him. He was almost to where the road climbed to take advantage of a low pass through a long diagonal ridgeline that cut across Hidden valley Road.

At the base of the ridgeline, the collision detection software outlined a Hispanic man near the side of the road by placing a red flashing box around him. The man leaned on a makeshift crutch and waved to flag the truck down. Raoul didn't normally pick up hitchhikers, but this man looked in good shape and wasn't carrying anything other than the crutch. Maybe a hiker who got hurt and now wanted a ride home before it became too dark?

Raoul decided to take a chance and stop, putting the truck on manual mode. By the time he saw the other eleven men with automatic weapons and body armor step out from behind rock cover and brush concealment, it was too late to do anything about it. "Madre de Dios!"

Raoul hadn't seen hijackers in a long time, not since the sovereign security companies took over the road security contracts. He pressed his panic button under the dash just as one of the men yanked open his door and piled in beside him.

Pedro pulled open the truck door and climbed in. He motioned two of his men to join him in the now crowded cab and sent the rest to quickly get in the back and hold the semi-trailer doors closed from the inside. The time for planning is past. Now time for action, Pedro thought. He normally anticipated action, but tonight he was filled with dread.

With no need to point his weapon directly at the truck driver, Pedro ordered "Start moving again. Back up to normal speed." as soon as his men were all aboard. Too long of a stop might raise suspicion. "What is your name?"

The truck driver started the truck moving on manual drive. "Raoul Dominguez. What is it you want? I have very little cargo on board. Certainly nothing portable and expensive, just big and bulky items."

"Never mind that, Raoul. Just do as you're told and you won't be hurt." The truck driver appeared to relax a little as Pedro called him by name.

The Sharper Security prison was only another three minutes up the road. As they approached, he noted nothing different from when they'd observed it from the bottom of the ridgeline. He picked out a spot closest to the base of the hill the prison rose atop and pointed, "Stop there." That's as good as it was going to get.

"I'm stopping." Raoul said, applying the brakes gently in order to reach the designated location. He looked up at the tall black stone walls of the prison surrounding the top half of the hill.

As the truck stopped, Pedro led his men in a burst out of the truck from the front and rear, looking for something to protect them as they spread out and charged across the 50 meters of loose pebbles and sand separating the road from the base of the hill. He found nothing; just bare rock and scrub brush so thin a jack rabbit couldn't hide behind it.

The running banditos made it to the base of the hill at a full run before small poles with curved tops rose silently and directly out of the hillside ahead in several staggered rows, a few meters between each one. Pedro recognized them immediately and involuntarily flinched in expectation before throwing himself to the ground.

Standing in for death, a voice from a loudspeaker addressed them, "You are trespassing on Sharper Security property. What you see on the side of the hill are multiple rows of directional mines, set to scrape the earth clear of your presence. If you aren't a complete idiot, you will now lay down your weapons and stand with your hands on your head. The first row of mines will detonate in 5... 4... 3... "

Pedro acted decisively the only way he could, shouting "We surrender. Camarados, lay down your arms!", laying his own weapons on the ground before the countdown reached zero, and then standing with his hands on his head. His men followed his example, albeit with a slightly slower reaction time.

From Sam's office in the center of the prison complex, where he could respond quickly to unexpected events from any direction, he continued watching the banditos' live surrender on a wall screen. As he'd expected, the invaders from La Raza Council made the right choice. Better captured than dead, he thought.

"Good choice. Stay as still as possible." he warned the banditos.

Sam had posted John just inside the north gate with a reaction squad of robots. Now he switched his audio to speak to him, "Proceed to the area east of the prison at the bottom of the hill. Send the robots to secure the attackers. They're quite adept at immobilizing prisoners safely."

"Aye, Aye, Sir" came the expected response from John. Sam was surprised John had never been tapped for OCS at Quantico. Good man. Someone's mistakes almost caused him to be wasted. Civilization couldn't afford that sort of waste. Not with all the scum out there.

"Stay behind the minefield until the prisoners are completely secured. I'd hate for one of them to try something stupid and get you killed. Think of the explaining I'd have to do to your relatives at the funeral." Sam realized John probably already knew that, but it didn't hurt to remind him not to be stupid.

"Explaining how I did something idiotic? They wouldn't find that surprising." John joked.

"No, explaining what an idiot I was to hire you and then let you get yourself killed. Besides, I hate funerals. Too expensive and they usually expect me to speak. I hate speaking engagements where I can't start with a good joke."

"I haven't seen a lot of people getting killed around here, but it's only my second day on the job. You expecting a body count?" John seemed concerned.

"Not if I can help it. The best war is a good clean one where you achieve your objectives with as little damage as possible. That's lesson number two. So far, so good, on this one. Read that book by Sun Tzu I've just sent you a link for when you have some time."

"Aye, Aye, Sir, the book will be read as duties allow. How many lessons are there?"

"No more than one a day. Gives you time to absorb them properly."

"Prisoners secured hand and foot by the bots. Please disarm the mines before I go collect their weapons." Back to business.

Sam verified from the cameras that all prisoners were secure and being transported back to the prison by the spider robots. He flipped a switch, causing the mines to retract back into the ground. "Mines secure. Kick a little dust back over the top of them again before you come in from collecting their weapons. No sense in making it too easy on the next group that thinks we're a target instead of a trap. I'll send a robot cart down to haul the weapons into the armory."

"Aye, Aye, Sir." As John started gathering weapons from the ground, Sam began directing the spider robots. One towards the road, another towing a cart towards John, most to a dorm to house their human cargo. Convenient, having your own prison.

Raoul watched as the banditos charged, stopped and were captured by Sharper Security. Didn't they realize there hadn't been a successful hijacking in years? And assaulting a prison! People didn't usually work so hard to get *into* a prison.

The mechanical spider leg tapping the back of his shoulder almost gave him a heart attack right there. Somehow, a spidery four foot tall metallic monster snuck into the cab of his truck from the other side while he watched the soldiers surrender. Madre de Dios!

The robot started repeating, "Follow me, Raoul Dominguez. You will not be harmed."

So much for finishing his deliveries tonight. He needed to tell his wife he'd be late. Possibly very late. She was going to be upset, even though it wasn't his fault!

A little later, Sam spoke, trying to hide a grin, "Maria, this is Raoul. I need you to find him a room for the night. After having his truck hijacked, I'm sure he's tired."

Maria stomped her foot on the tile floor of the orphanage's entryway, "That floozy Michelle called for you again. Don't you have an electronic answering machine? You know I don't like her."

Raoul just stood in the entranceway and twisted his hands, obviously wondering what he'd gotten himself into now.

Sam nodded placating, "I don't like her anymore, either. You always talk to her because she's got some trick to get past my computerized screener. She knows it's set to reject all her calls. Somehow, she gets connected to the hardline phone system here anyway. I wish you'd let me just get you a mobile phone like everyone else in the world has."

"You going to call her back so she stops calling me? I run an orphanage; I'm not your secretary."

"I'll deal with her later. Right now, I have bigger worries. Policía La Raza sent a team to attack the prison. Please find a place for Raoul?"

Maria flounced back her long dark hair, "When are you going to stop bringing me stray men? I run a home for children, not adults. Maricopa has hotels, you know! You probably haven't even fed him yet!"

"I need him close by. Besides, why would I take him to a hotel when I know you still have several empty rooms in the orphanage? He's been through a lot today, so be nice."

She huffed. "I'm always nice. Nicer to you than you deserve. I'll put him in one of the staff rooms. We have a vacancy there." Maria turned and started down the hallway.

Sam gestured for Raoul to hurry up and follow her, "My home is just up the ridgeline, if you need anything, but I'm sure Maria will take good care of you. Just don't make her mad. You don't want to see her when she's upset."

Chapter 5 - Day Five

Cartegna Lane, Maricopa, Arizona Zone

Morning

Evie didn't know if she could face it. Riding back home with John Parkur to pick up some of her things, she paled at the idea of seeing the reality. The reality of her destroyed home.

Living in the home on Cartegna Lane was new to Evie, but anticipation for the condition of Hamish's carefully preserved possessions made her pulse race and her chest carry a thousand bricks. She started quietly sobbing, hoping John wouldn't notice.

John smiled nervously at her while driving the last short block before the turn on to Cartegna Lane, "Are you sure you're going to be ok with this? We can have it sorted out without you."

Evie tried to take a deep breath and smile, only partially succeeding, "I can do this. I want to see what it looks like." She took another breath, "I mean, I don't want to see what it looks like, but I need to see what it looks like." She wasn't sure what she wanted, but she knew she was strong enough to collect a few things from the ruins of her house.

As John made the last turn, Evie caught sight of the ruined home with an intake of breath. "Not much to look at." he commented.

She was absolutely devastated. Everything destroyed. The house collapsed down on top of autocab wreckage. Her clothes, furniture, everything scattered or in pieces.

The worst was the garage. Evie's view blocked by wreckage and rubble, by wrecked autocabs, she couldn't even see the things stored in the garage. Hamish's things, carefully preserved after he died. Everything she had left of him. What was she going to do?

John stopped and parked the large black and white Sharper Security pickup truck with her side to the sidewalk. For a moment, she thought he'd parked facing the wrong way on the road.

Evie was in America and she could do this. She took another deep breath and stepped cautiously down out of the truck. Well, not much home left behind. Her side still hurt a bit, but not as much as her painful breathing while standing and looking over the ruins of her home. The ruins of all her worldly possessions.

John came around the front of the truck in a hurry, "Are you sure you can manage? I would have helped you step down." He looked very concerned for her welfare. How sweet. She could do worse, as protectors went.

"I can manage, but thank you. I'm so pleased you were able to bring me out to get some of my things. Let's get started straight away. I'm not sure how long I can manage, as shafted as I feel." Evie looked over the smashed home, collapsed in on itself and a bunch of damaged autocabs. She felt like collapsing, herself; felt like she was the wrecked home.

John seemed dubious about the whole idea, "I don't think you should be climbing around in that mess in your condition."

"I'm all at sixes and sevens. You simply walk about the wreck and I'll point at things I want brought back with us. NHS wouldn't let me out about on the street in my condition."

Looking around for any other threats, John proceeded toward the large pile of rubbish.

Evie followed, and then pointed at the large trash can still standing at the curb, miraculously missed by the autocabs, "It seems the dustbin man hasn't been about. Quite the mess."

John seemed to notice the big plastic wheeled trashcan for the first time. "Hmm.... That should have been picked up already. Perhaps the police tape on the street scared them away. No matter, Sam says we'll have a dumpster in here in the next few days, along with a rented robot crew to sort out the rubble and the personal items not worth saving. No offense intended, Ma'am."

She could see reality for herself. There wasn't going to be much worth saving and the impact was finally starting to fully hit her. "Why don't you start around the top, in the front? Most of my immediate personal needs would have been in the loo."

John seemed glad to have something to do. "Yes, Ma'am." He said, as he began to clamber across the wreckage, leaving Evie with her thoughts.

This wasn't what she'd expected in her new life. Oh, she'd joked about adventure, but really, this was quite enough. She wanted relaxation, perhaps a bit of gardening. Safety and security, not standing in the hot sun trying to salvage a small piece of her life to take back to a prison hospital with her.

Evie pointed at some toiletries and nodded to John to confirm he should bring them back to load into the truck. Most of that stuff was replaceable, but she was so new to the area she didn't know where to even get it. She supposed Sam or John could tell her, although men were rarely practical about those sorts of things. Hamish had never been. She was used to knowing where to go, what to do next, to being in charge of her fate. Here she was away from friends, with no one to rely on other than her hired security. Thank goodness that had been in her contract for the home, otherwise she didn't know what she'd do. She missed Hamish.

"How about these boxes?" John wanted to know, holding one up to show her.

She nodded and pointed to the truck. Lucky she hadn't fully unpacked already. "Brilliant. Any other boxes you find would be wonderful as well." Having John around as a dogsbody was working out, but it was daft to think she could replace Hamish with anyone.

Losing someone close to you was devastating, really. Even though she worked, Hamish had still taken care of her in the most important ways. Oh, she took care of him as well, but when she needed someone, as she needed someone now, Hamish had always been that someone.

She kept thinking he'd come around the corner and say it was all a joke. He'd been famous for his jokes. Now all she had of him was buried in rubble and run over by smashed autocabs. Really quite stressful, she cried inside.

"Are you ok?" John seemed to have snuck up on her while she was internally distracted.

She brushed back a tear, "I'm all right. I don't suppose you can try and recover a bit of my husband Hamish's things? It just tears me up to know they're buried in there somewhere."

"Where would they be? I can dig around a bit. We aren't on a schedule."

"I was storing them in the garage. Probably in the middle there, as far as the autocabs made it before the whole place collapsed on top of them." Why did I put them in the garage?

"In the middle of the largest pile of rubble you mean?" John asked.

"Yes. I know that's the worst place to go digging around, but I can't bear to think they're lost forever." A safe would have been better. A big steel box in a safe, with me carrying the only key. Why did Hamish have to be a hero? Why couldn't he have just gone along like the rest of us?

The dubious tone in John's voice returned, "I'll see what I can do. Eventually it'll all be sorted out and what can be salvaged will be." John finished loading what he'd already found into the back of the truck and made his way cautiously back to the ruins of the home, looking for a safe way into the middle of the pile.

Hamish had fancied himself an action man. That was the real trouble with today's society. Too many people looking to take the responsibility of the world on their shoulders, not thinking about the other people who depend on them. Family should come first, not job.

Why did Hamish have to try and stand up to those bloody rioters, anyway?

John returned holding a slightly torn and stained men's dress shirt, "This is all I could reach. The rubble is too precarious in that area to be able to get much closer right now."

"We'll have to wait until the robots have a go at it." She sniffled. She deserved better than to have Hamish go and die on her, and then to have to come all the way out here just to have her home destroyed.

He drove down the road in his black Camaro, speeding and taking corners as quickly as he could without drawing unwanted attention. In the video feed displayed within his glasses, he watched as Evie stood by and let the Rez Indian climb over the ruins of her home. He'd been hoping for a break like this. Hoping she'd come outside the protective walls of the Sharper Security prison.

As he turned a sharp corner, he reached out to keep the high powered rifle leaning up against the passenger seat from shifting. With a gyro stabilized, top of the line, intelligent sniper rifle, as long as he had a few moments to aim, moments for the expert system in the scope to adjust for wind and distance to his aim point, he wouldn't miss from anything less than a mile. All he needed was a clear line of sight and a solid place to rest the stabilization system on. There weren't any real high points around to use, but the top of a single story house down at the other end of the street would work just fine.

Anticipating she'd eventually return to her home, he'd posted a calibrated aiming point right on the street sign just outside her driveway. The target he'd pasted up was just over head height. He already had the roof of the house he'd fire from chosen. Two alternate locations, actually, where one set of the neighbors worked days and the other nights, giving him a secure firing location no matter the time of day. He could park behind either and use the backyard block walls as cover for his car and as a ladder to reach the roof.

He had it all figured out. Her payment was just beginning.

John turned to circle around the piles of rubble again, "Let me keep looking. Maybe there's another way into there that isn't as dangerous." He could tell how much Hamish's things meant to Evie. To him, they were just the miscellaneous remaining possessions of a man with no more earthly use for them. He'd never understood why people relied so much on possessions. Of course, he'd never had many. Oh, his father and mother had plenty, but between living in the Marine Corps and then back in his parent's home, he'd never had much of a chance for material accumulation.

The words she used sometimes confused him. Sixes and sevens. Who even knew what that meant? He wished she'd speak English. He had a Filipino buddy who'd been easier to understand. Too bad Cockbay didn't make it.

Evie looked like she was going to start crying again, "That would be most appreciated. It's really quite stressful."

John continued looking for a safe way through the rubble. The falling walls and smashed roof tiles formed places that looked like tunnels, but he knew from experience that it was more precarious than it looked. A shift of a fallen wall or some beams caused by someone's weight moving around was enough to flatten anyone stupid enough to be caught digging around inside. You could move piece of rubble to get behind it and in the process change the pressure on something else that was actually supporting where you were standing. Live action Jenga with your life in the balance. He'd spent plenty of time in third world war torn countries, digging through the remains of buildings hit by a mortar or a car bomb. Enough time to realize retrieving Evie's possessions was more dangerous than it looked.

Marko and Cockbay. They'd been out of his thoughts for a couple of days now, a new record. He'd been too busy staying professionally worried about Evie. Maybe he'd just needed something else to focus on for a while. Watching Evie deal with her grief wasn't easy, but it was safer than dealing with his own memories.

John looked around to make sure Evie was still tracking him, and then ducked into a section of collapsed building near where he thought her dead husband's belongings resided. Crawling through a tunnel created by a door and the remains of a wall, he reached an area within the garage inaccessible from the other side.

Let's see. A racquet. Too bulky, unlikely to be much value. A black velvet box, wider than both his hands, still intact, maybe some jewelry or something else valuable. Perfect. John tossed the box ahead of him towards the exit for the tunnel and then crawled after it. Just as he reached the edge and started to stand up, the rubble shifted a few feet beneath him, giving him a distinct sliding out of control feeling.

John kept his balance long enough to jump off the pile. Once it settled, he grabbed the keepsake box and walked back over to Evie. He decided the box would have to be the last thing he recovered. Too risky. Better to let the robots designed for this kind of work do it.

"Ah. Hamish's decorations and medallions. I'm glad you were able to find those." Evie said. Looked more like she could use some fry bread and a drink.

John took a deep breath. He couldn't believe he was bringing this up, but she seemed so upset. "You don't look very glad right now. I know what it's like to lose someone close to you. I still think about what I could've done to keep them alive." Maybe she could use the knowledge she wasn't the only one to ever go through a loss like that.

Evie cocked her head slightly, "Who?"

He didn't really want to think about it. "I was in the Philippines with the Marines. Our mission was to train a local army unit, provide some leadership, some examples of how to run a modern army. Marko and Cockbay."

"Cockbay? Unusual name." She could hardly speak.

"Oh, Cockbay was Filipino. His real name was Caacbay. C-A-A-C-B-A-Y" he spelled out for her, "but we all just called him Cockbay. One of those nicknames that just sticks. Marko's name was really just Mark, but Marko seemed to fit him better. I guess everyone had some sort of nickname. Everyone who was around for long, anyway. Some of the short timers, they never got nicknames."

Evie paused, took a breath, then ventured, "What happened?"

"Cockbay was originally from the Philippines, still had some family there. He spoke the language the best. Marko was his best buddy, but we were all in the same fireteam. Your fireteam is like your family. We did everything together. I could count on one hand how many times we were more than 50 meters away from each other in the two years I spent in country."

Evie nodded.

John lost himself in the memories. "I was the team leader, carried a grenade launcher. Cockbay scouted, Marko had an M27 automatic rifle. Irish Danny was Marko's assistant. Carried the extra ammo, that sort of thing. We were in the back country, patrolling villages. You know, shacks made from aluminum sheeting and plywood were the high-end. Nothing that was supposed to be too dangerous. Just training. Squad with three fireteams and a Sergeant goes along with a Philippine company to pretend there are bad guys out in the trees or in a village and practice how to maneuver. One day, we were supposed to setup a fake ambush, make the Philippine company keep an eye out for us. Sarge split the fireteams up. I was senior team lead, so I took our team one way. Sarge went another way with the other team. The plan was to wander through the area enough to lose the locals and then meet back up to lay an ambush just before they stopped for the night. Sarge figured they'd be tired of walking and watching the weeds about then."

"Cockbay wanted to take a detour to see some family. A nearby village was supposed to have one of his cousins or something in it. I figured we had all day to kill, no particular path we had to take, so why not?"

"I found out why not. We all did. Cockbay walked into his cousin's village, nice and easy. Sauntered in, really. Why not, he wasn't a local, was a big bad war hero from the states. I trailed behind him a bit. Marko and Danny came in from the left side. We weren't totally ignoring protocol, but I let them get way too casual."

"A local terrorist group took over the village the night before. Planned to make our training exercise more exciting or something. Show they could hit where they weren't expected."

"They caught Cockbay with the first burst. He never got a shot off. Marko laid into them with his light machine gun. Cut right through the buildings, but they got him next. Danny and I hit the dirt, retreated a bit. Way more of them than of us."

"I radioed for air support and we dug in from two sides, kept them pinned down so they didn't take off. Not that they couldn't see they had us outnumbered. None of them wanted to be the first to die coming after us, though. Small village. I could see almost all the way around it. Between us, we had all the edges covered, for the few minutes it mattered. Felt like days. Gunships pasted the village. Afterward, we counted sixteen dead combatants, not including Cockbay and Marko. Dead terrorists. Muslim guerrillas. The shacks ..." his voice cracked up a little.

"The shacks had another dozen villagers. Old men, women, children. I'm still not sure how many were already dead, killed when they took over the village, and how many the gunships got. We didn't count. The guerrillas were hiding in the shacks. You couldn't really see them, just gun barrels and flashes of firing."

"I've gotten over the villagers. They were dead as soon as the guerrillas took over the place. They'd have killed the rest as soon as they were done with it as a base. But Cockbay and Marko... It was my job to keep them from doing something stupid, like walk into that village without a care in the world."

"I talked to Cockbay's Mom after they pulled us back stateside. She didn't understand. Oh, she understood the Philippines. They had gotten out. Gotten a new life for her family. She didn't understand how I let her baby go back and get killed there. How come he was dead and I wasn't." John shook his head. "Neither do I, really."

"I got bone spurs in my wrist. Got out. But I still think of Marko and Cockbay. Especially Cockbay. I can still see the look on his Mother's face. Still see him walking into that village. I used to see it every night. Now it's less often. You never get over that sort of thing."

"So yeah, I know what it's like to lose someone close to you."

Evie was sobbing. Maybe that wasn't the best idea, to tell her all that. He had to tell someone, though.

"Let's go back to the truck." he added, putting his arm around her shoulders.

He lay on the red tile roof, focused in on the target he'd pasted as an aiming point. He imagined what it would be like to put the scope on her kneecap, make her remember every time she took a step, but that wasn't the plan today.

He gently squeezed the trigger, knowing his aim was true. He could hear the crack of the bullet's passage echo off the nearby homes and block walls.

Fire and move. He grabbed up the rifle and stabilizer and hustled down the roofline toward the rear wall he'd used as a ladder.

Hidden Valley Road, Maricopa, Arizona Zone

About that same time

Pedro watched the steel door open from his uncomfortable chair. Sam stepped through the doorway. He seemed to be paying attention to the video in his glasses, but Pedro could tell he had at least one eye for him.

"Hey man." he said defiantly, "I don't have anything to say to you."

"I know your family is back in La Raza Council. I know you think anything you say will get them hurt. I'm not here to hurt them." Sam seemed concerned, not angry.

"What does a gabacho know about mi familia? Mi familia es todo para mi." *My family means everything to me.*

"I know a lot about family. A lot about motivation." Sam smiled as he crossed the floor towards Pedro, "I know most men will do anything to protect their family. Even follow idiotic orders to get themselves killed. Attacking a prepared position on foot across open ground? Even your men knew that was stupid. A waste. What was the point?"

"Sometimes you have to sacrifice for what you believe in." Pedro knew he hadn't a choice.

"Sacrifice so that Lieutenant Garcia doesn't look like he isn't doing anything about Shortee Tejada? Or sacrifice so your family can live as the privileged family of a Policía La Raza soldier?"

Pedro decided he'd said enough. No answers, that's what they'd always said. Once you start talking about anything, it was easier to keep talking about things you shouldn't. Things that could get your family hurt, if the wrong people found out. And they always found out.

"Do you sacrifice when you threaten other men's families? Or are you above that work yourself, just keeping your mouth shut?"

Pedro sat tight-lipped.

Sam sighed, "It doesn't really matter. I know why you're here. I knew you were coming. Knew when you crossed I-80. Watched you as you drove up the road in the truck. Waited for you to demonstrate your intentions. There's nothing you can tell me about this trip of yours that matters. You're lucky to be alive. Next time I catch you or your men anywhere that Sharper Security protects, you won't hear my voice out of a speaker. You won't hear anything again. Think of that when you're making your next career move."

Pedro watched as Sam exited the cell. It sounded like his team was going home, never to return. He hoped Garcia didn't take it out on them too badly, but even el Teniente knew there wasn't much of a chance for success. A suicide mission ending badly, but with everyone surviving.

He suspected Garcia's preference would be for Pedro's team to be dead. No one to contradict whatever story Garcia told and he could show their corpses as evidence of Policía La Raza's commitment to retrieve Shortee at any cost.

He knew Garcia wouldn't be happy with Pedro's surrender, but he couldn't take that out on Pedro's family, could he?

Raoul watched on the wall screen in Sam's office as Sam left Pedro's isolation cell. He didn't really want to think about what life must be like in La Raza Council, even for a soldier, with their extra privileges. He almost felt sorry for the soldiers who'd hijacked his truck.

Sam came in from the hallway and took the seat behind his desk, "No point in pushing him. He's already in enough trouble back home and I already know plenty about what they were here for. Their whole bandito story, spontaneously deciding to rob a prison using your truck? They all know that doesn't hold any water around here."

"What will you do with them?" Raoul asked.

"Give them back, as part of a suitable exchange. It wasn't their idea; they just almost got killed for it. They won't be back around here and Policía La Raza will punish them much more than I ever would. Besides, they can't afford a fine, but La Raza will ransom them, pretending they will be punished for their actions, if only so the next group of poor shmucks they give a stupid order to will do what they say."

"What can we do about them? La Raza, I mean." Raoul had never given much thought to the people living in La Raza Council. He mostly just passed through.

Sam laughed, "Us? Not much. They'll stay this way until the people who live there notice the rest of Arizona Zone is leaving them behind. Then they'll either pack up and leave, or else throw the bums out. They could all decide to contract with Sharper Security tomorrow, pay us to protect them from Policía La Raza, or anyone else. Sure, we'd have to charge a lot at first, but we'd get the job done. No, if they're suffering in La Raza Council, it's either because they want to live that way, having bought into blaming someone else, or because they don't know anything better. They have a choice. At least some of them must have access to the online world, access to see there are better solutions out there."

"You make me almost feel bad for the men who hijacked my truck. Sorry I pushed the panic button." Raoul frowned.

Sam smiled again and stood to pat Raoul on the back, "You pushing that panic button likely saved their lives. We knew they were around, but not exactly where and how they'd attack. Knowing they were coming in your truck let me arrange everything just perfectly, just in time. If they'd come running up like that, but completely unexpected, let's just say they may not have had an opportunity to surrender. The automated systems around here are very good at recognizing a threat when it's as obvious as a bunch of guys carrying weapons and charging up a hill."

"I see what you mean. I still have deliveries to make. When can I leave?"

"You can make your deliveries now, but I'm afraid you're going to have to come back here afterwards with an empty truck."

"I too, have a family I must get back to." Raoul protested.

"Let's talk about what you can do to help these men and their families. Once I arrange for a ransom, they're going to need a ride back to La Raza, and since you managed to carry them here..."

Madre de Dios! Raoul's wife was going to kill him when he finally got home. He'd already had to explain why he didn't come home *last* night!

Rita Road, South Tucson, La Raza Council

About that same time

Garcia had thought reporting directly to el Jefe after his most recent promotion was going to really enhance his career. Instead, it appeared likely to end his life, or send him to the mines. He'd covered up last night's debacle as much as he could, gave el Jefe deniability with the council people, but he also knew he couldn't ignore Sam Harper's calls much longer.

Once Garcia took Sam's call, he knew he'd have to make a decision, and because this was his operation, he was going to have to deal with the consequences. Strategically, there just wasn't a good way to attack Sam and free Shorty Tejada. Ideally, he'd arrange for a situation to entice Sam to come to him. To get Sam away from his warning sensors and fixed defenses.

Having Shorty in a gabacho prison was very bad. Getting Garcia's men captured, not killed, but captured, was almost as bad. Their surrender reflected poorly not only on his planning, but also on their strength of will and by reflection, his leadership.

He'd watched, screaming into his video display, as Pedro was the first one to surrender. Garcia knew Pedro's men didn't have a chance to do anything but surrender or shortly be shredded into little pieces upon the ground, but no one else had that video yet. Perhaps he could edit it to show Pedro surrendering and ordering his men to surrender, but remove the obvious threats. It would still reflect poorly on him that his subordinate had done such a thing, but everyone knew there were mal bicho, *bad bugs*, in every pile. It's not as if Garcia recruited Pedro for Policía La Raza personally.

It would be ideal if Pedro never returned, but he'd better secure his family just in case Pedro came back and needed a reminder not to contradict Garcia's version of events.

Garcia asked his phone to connect him to the Policía La Raza station nearest Pedro's home. The sergeant there owed him a few little favors. Time to collect.

Cartegna Lane, Maricopa, Arizona Zone

About that same time

John put his arm around Evie to help her back towards the black and white Sharper Security truck parked at the curb. As he turned her towards the truck, he saw a glint of light on a roof where there wasn't one before. Light reflected from a rifle scope?

"Sniper!" automatically came out of his mouth as he shoved Evie toward the ground behind the truck. Too late, he thought, as he heard the crack of a supersonic rifle round and the smack of an impact almost simultaneously. Once you hear the sonic boom, it's too late, the bullet is already past, he remembered. He followed Evie to the ground anyway.

"AHHH!" Evie screamed. She obviously wasn't registering things yet.

John looked around from the ground, scanning the area. He couldn't see the roof location he'd picked out as the source of the bullet. That was good, meant the shooter likely couldn't see them behind the truck, either.

Evie trembled on the ground, holding her side tightly and breathing rapidly. "Hey, what?"

John's next thought was to call Sam using the encrypted, frequency hopping radio he'd earlier admired. "Sniper at Evie's house. We've got the truck between us and a possible position."

"Sending backup to cover the area. See if you can get into the truck and get out of there. The truck is armored, but keep Evie below the window line anyway. Watch out for rocket and missile launchers. Hit the big blue button if you see one. Otherwise, you should be ok while inside the truck and moving." John appreciated the brief instructions.

"Let's go. Into the truck." He pulled Evie toward the passenger door.

"Umm... ok." Evie replied, but John mostly had to drag her across the sidewalk to the truck while she winced in pain at every movement. She didn't look hit. He'd seen someone hit by a sniper rifle before. Made a big hole coming out.

John glanced at himself as he climbed into the truck, pulling Evie in after him. He wasn't hit either. Sometimes the adrenaline could mask the pain at first.

"Stay low," he ordered as he climbed across the cab of the truck to the driver's side, "Under the window level." John started the truck and made a quick U-turn, away from the wrecked home and the sniper's perch, toward the safety of the Sharper Security prison.

Evie lay on the floor and bench seat on the right side of the truck's cab, sobbing, "Why me? What did I do to deserve all this?"

Hidden Valley Road, Maricopa, Arizona Zone

A few minutes later

Sam watched live video from aerial drones over Maricopa neighborhoods as John and Evie passed through them on the way back to the prison. He decided he'd obviously been too complacent about keeping an eye on the area. Flying drones cost money, though, and when John and Evie left, he didn't think someone would be laying in ambush for them. He should have considered that Evie's enemy may have lost her and been watching her house in order to find her again.

The truck John was driving Evie back to the Sharper Security prison in had reached John Wayne Parkway when Sam noticed a notification icon on his screen. The security lawyers at Flag Health Center had responded to his request for parking lot video and his video analysis routines had identified something that fit his parameters in the video they'd sent.

Sam called up the video and watched as Pierre's son Edmond exited the black Camaro and made his way into the hospital. Sure, it could be just a coincidence, but with the other ties Pierre had to Evie, Sam didn't think so. He was going to have another talk with Pierre.

A request to open the vehicle gate was automatically generated as John's company truck approached. After checking to make sure it was still John driving, Sam approved the request and started toward the hallway. Time to get more details from John on what really happened out there.

Cowtown Road, Casa Grande, Arizona Zone

An hour later

Pierre looked up as Edmond pushed open Agence Sécurité's front door and burst through the doorway. Teenagers, always in a hurry.

"I'm sorry, Dad. I have to go." Edmond spoke rapidly while he walked behind the counter and started pulling things off shelves.

"You just arrived here. Your shift starts soon. What is ze rush? Tell me, what do you need with all that?" He really needed to teach Pierre some manners, but without a mother, Edmond had to make do with Pierre's habits while growing up.

"I have to leave. I don't want to put you in danger, and I think I just screwed up. I should have never gone there in person." Edmond continued to pack a black duffle bag with expensive security equipment.

What was Edmond talking about? "What is this in regard to? You know you can talk to me. If you are in trouble, ze Agence is the place for you."

Edmond stopped his frantic activity for a moment, "I know you remember Evie. You raised me with the story of what happened to my parents. I've just been paying back some of what she did to me, that's all, but now I've made an enemy out of Sharper Security. You've taught me well. I know enough to know you can't keep them out of here. I'm not even sure you'd try." Edmond frowned, "I'm not even sure you should try, if I stick around. I don't want you or anyone who works for you to get killed because of my decisions."

So it was Edmond who'd been harassing Evie. Pierre had wondered ever since Sam brought up the black Camaro, but he hadn't talked to him about it yet. He told himself it was because he was waiting for him to come in for his shift, but maybe it was because he didn't want to bring up an old and painful subject yet again. "Don't be the goat. You do not have to do this. You have not killed anyone, I presume?"

"No, but I'm sure they're going to take it seriously now. I missed Evie on purpose, just wanted to scare her, but they won't know that. She's probably telling them right now about how frightened she is." Edmond placed a few more items in his duffle bag.

Pierre hadn't ever seen Edmond this serious before. Oh, sometimes he brooded, but usually he was lighthearted, joking around. "I can pay whatever fine is assessed. I have good a legal consultant, one of ze best. We will think of something. You should stay right here. I will call Sam and negotiate. He can be trusted to not do anything foolish."

Edmond shook his head, "You don't understand. I'm not going to give myself up. They'll have to catch me. This isn't the end, it's just the beginning. I joined you in Agence Sécurité because I wanted to protect people. People like my parents, who didn't do anything wrong. That's all I was doing. Evie needs to learn you can't just kill people, destroy their home, and then get away with it. I don't want to live in a world where that's what happens, and no one does anything about it. They were my parents. It's my job to do something about it."

"That was long ago," Pierre said, "your parents are dead. I know Evie hurt your family when she wouldn't listen, but revenge will not bring your parents back. Stay here. Ze Agence can work this out with Sam. Let me protect you."

"I can't. Not this time. Thank you for bringing me up, for telling me what really happened, but this is something I have to do." Edmond finished his packing and gave Pierre a hug, "You're the only parent I've known and I love you, but don't try to stop me."

Pierre squeezed him back and didn't want to let go, "You are, my only son, my fiston. I don't need another. I wish you to reconsider. Where will you go?"

"South, to La Raza Council territory. They have no reason to like Sam Harper right now. I can hide there and plan my next move."

"Fais gaffe, Policía La Raza has have no reason to like you. I wish you will stay, but you are an adult. I will not make you, will not arrest you."

"I know. Thank you for understanding. Now I have to leave. I'm going to need a head start." Edmond headed for the door.

"Un moment. If you must go, take some of the hombres in the holding cells with you. Perhaps they will buy some protection from La Raza Council. In the meantime, I'll talk with Sam. Maybe we can make a deal." Pierre thought he could work something out with Sam. They'd done a lot of business over the years.

"Thanks again, Dad. I'll take some prisoners from that land rocket gang with me. Go hide in the office. I'll tell them it's a jailbreak, that I'm rebelling or something and want them to help me with Policía La Raza."

Pierre thought that Edmond always was the smart one in the family, but not today, "Adieu, son. Don't be the goat. Put revenge behind you." He turned to hide in his own office.

Rita Road, South Tucson, La Raza Council

About that same time

Garcia called Sam, selecting full audio and video for the call. He wanted to be able to see his face while they negotiated. Not that Garcia had much to work with, but if the filthy gabacho didn't want to trade Policía La Raza's men back, they could sit in prison with Shortee Tejada. Better than being here with an angry el Jefe.

Sam appeared on Garcia's screen as the call connected. "Afternoon, Lieutenant Garcia. I see you decided to return my call."

Garcia pasted a smile on his face, "Señor Harper. I am calling to arrange the return of a very valued member of our community, Shortee Tejada. What can I do for you to make that happen?"

Sam shook his head, "Unfortunately, Shortee Tejada is serving a prison sentence and I have an obligation to ensure he serves all of it. As his offense was not against Sharper Security, his obligations are not ones I am contractually able to release. However, if you would like to send him some comforts from home, I can make sure he receives them."

The man was infuriating. Didn't he know the way the world worked? Men with power like Shortee's father, they didn't play by the same rules as everyone else. Let Sam think he won this round. "If we can't come to an agreement on Shortee, let's discuss some other men. I understand you are holding some tourists from La Raza Council? Some men in the wrong place at the wrong time?"

Sam cut off his instinctive laugh, "Tourists, eh? It must be dangerous in La Raza Council, if your tourists come with body armor and automatic weapons."

Garcia did his best to look innocent, "Did they kill anyone? Damage any property? My understanding is that they agreed to follow your orders, as soon as they realized they had accidentally stumbled into the wrong field."

"Trespassing, certainly. You also forget they hijacked a truck, held the driver at gunpoint. Kidnapping and truck-jacking are serious offenses. Very valuable cargo in that truck. High security area they trespassed in."

"You haven't held a trial yet, have you? No conviction for anything yet? Perhaps we can save you some expense and try them here in La Raza Council. They are, after all, apparently our citizens."

"They lacked any official identification, but my records indicate they actually belong to your organization, Policía La Raza." Sam seemed amused by the whole conversation.

"Personnel files being private, I am certainly unable to confirm your information." Metete un pelo en el culo, gabacho, Garcia thought at Sam. "What about the truck allegedly involved in this incident?"

"I've reached an understanding with the owner of the truck in question to represent him in this matter. He's signed his claim over to Sharper Security. As for the trespassing, that was against Sharper Security directly. So happily, we can deal directly and solve this whole matter ourselves." Sam smiled.

The negotiation wasn't going as well as Garcia had hoped. He needed a beer. "What do you want?"

Sam ticked off his wish list, "The cost of delays in the truck shipment, penalties paid to the cargo recipients, recompense to the truck driver, expenses for defending Sharper Security prison from these men, punitive damages to ensure they never attempt this sort of thing again. I understand Policía La Raza is having issues with paying in hard currency. Ten pounds of gold should cover it."

That much gold? Ávido! Garcia would have to get el Jefe involved. Shaking his head, he responded, "Too much. In return, you propose what, to agree to let Policía La Raza try these men solely in our court?"

Sam smiled, "That's my purchase price for assigning my claims against them to you, or whomever you designate. After that, they are your problem. I'll throw in delivery to your office in Tucson. You can pay the driver."

Ten pounds of gold? The driver wouldn't make it out of La Raza Council alive, even if Garcia did nothing to stop him. Might be nice to get el Jefe to supply the gold, and then keep it himself, if he could work out a way to do it without discovery. If Pedro was killed in an exchange gone bad, so much the better. No need to be obvious about his plans. "Too much, I say. We don't need your claims assignment, just a full settlement and release and the men delivered. I want to talk with the leader of these men, Pedro. Make sure all is as you say."

"One minute and I'll connect you." Sam's image disappeared from the screen, replaced by an image of Pedro in a cell, obviously from a surveillance camera. Sam's voice came again, "Speak and he'll hear you. The microphones in his cell will pick up any reply."

Garcia tried to think of what to say with Sam listening, "Pedro. This is Policía Lieutenant Garcia. I understand you are a La Raza Council Citizen being held in the Sharper Security prison." Admit to nothing, Garcia thought. A sound policy most of the time.

Pedro looked up at where the speaker was presumably hidden, "El Teniente Garcia. I hear you. I am from La Raza Council."

Pedro seemed to understand the conversation was being monitored. "How are they treating you and the men you were traveling with?" No need to get specific.

"Estamos bien. I see the other men during our exercise period. We would all like to go home and see our families."

So they are all still there and Pedro wants to know what's happening to his family. "La familia es lo más importante. Your family is safe and under the protection of Policía La Raza. Señor Harper accuses you of many serious crimes. Have you confessed these crimes?"

"I have not had the opportunity to speak with Señor Harper in detail. None of us has done any talking with the local authorities."

Good. No hard evidence for Sharper Security to hold over them later, or distribute to his enemies to make Garcia look bad. "We are arranging for the return of you and the other men to La Raza Council. It will be very expensive. Perhaps you have some relatives who will be able to assist you in paying Policía La Raza back after you have returned. Maybe pagar a plazos." *Pay in installments.*

Pedro thought over the implied threat for a second, "I am sure we will all be able to make you happy when we return home."

Pedro sounded like he would go along, Garcia thought, but he simply knew too much. Something would still have to be arranged after Pedro returned. "I am grateful for your decision to cooperate."

The screen blanked and then Sam appeared again, "So, ten pounds to settle all claims regarding the men? When do you want delivery? I must warn you, if you refuse delivery, I will still expect payment. I am sending you a filled in contract. You'll just need to file it with a bonding authority."

Garcia sighed; this was going to cost him many accumulated favors, "I will arrange it with my superiors. Send the men tomorrow. I will notify you tonight when all is arranged."

Hidden Valley Road, Maricopa, Arizona Zone

About that same time

John watched Sam disconnect the call with Garcia. "What was all that about Pedro's family?"

"Garcia was telling him they've rounded up their families and reminding him to keep his men all quiet. Passing that message is part of Garcia's price for arranging the exchange. They'll be home tomorrow night, no harm done."

"Now that you have the prisoner swap arranged, can I go after Edmond? Between the hospital video and the street video on Murphy road showing him leaving the area around Evie's house in a hurry right after the sniper attack, you know he's got to be our guy." John wondered why Sam was hesitant to take immediate action. He usually seemed pretty decisive.

"Edmond may not be as easy to capture as you think. Let's call Pierre. See what he has to say about it all. I don't want any of us to go near Agence de Sécurité in person until we know what to expect."

John thought he knew what to expect, but Sam had a lot more experience in this business. "I'll step to the side again so he only sees you. Thanks for letting me watch."

"You may have to deal with these men for me someday. Someday soon, even. Good for you to get to know them. It's good to know your friends, but if you want to survive, you need to know your enemies better than their best friend does. Learn how they think. That's lesson number three."

John stepped out of camera range to watch Sam open a video call to Pierre. The call connected, showing Pierre inside the Agence de Sécurité office.

"You can't have him, Sam. Ça salope killed his parents, but she can't have Edmond." John didn't speak French, but Pierre seemed upset.

"You want to explain that, Pierre?" Sam leaned back in his chair. His voice was calm and level by comparison.

"Evie sat there and did nothing when I told her it was ze wrong apartment. She let them destroy it. Let them kill his parents. It's a miracle Edmond survived."

"You're saying the apartment destroyed in Paris was Edmond's family?"

"As a baby, Edmond was in ze apartment when ze charges exploded. He was protected enough to survive, even if his parents did not. After they died, he would have been brought up as an orphan, but I adopt him instead. You do not understand Sam, she is evil. Oh, she seems to be very nice, but she was indifferent to their deaths. For her, it was all a video game, a pretend story where people don't matter. Subjects A and B in her memos to higher authority, not real people." Pierre seemed to blame Evie, but John thought he felt at least partially responsible as well, adopting Edmond like that.

"Well, that certainly explains a lot about what's been going on around here. Did Edmond admit responsibility for the attacks to you?"

"Edmond is a foolish young man. He needs revenge for his parents." John thought Pierre's response was not exactly a direct response to the question, but not much of a denial, either.

"Pierre, I can't let him continue in this. Sharper Security must bring him to trial for his actions." Sam was holding firm.

"I won't have him hurt. He is too young and this is not his fault. All he has of his parents is that silver cross." Pierre just seemed concerned for Edmond's safety. That explained his willingness to talk with Sam about it all. John considered that some water cannons might come in handy for dealing with Edmond.

"You know me, Pierre. I won't harm him unless he forces me to, but I will bring him in. Would save us all a lot of effort if he surrendered, or if Agence de Sécurité brought him in. Reduce the risk to everyone." Sam didn't seem to be looking forward to a fight.

"I tried, but he has decided to run south instead. He foolishly believes it will make him harder to find." Pierre just made it much easier to find Edmond. John wondered why.

"With Shortee Tejada locked up here because of Edmond's arrest, he may be in more danger in La Raza Council than in my prison." Sam's comment may have just explained the why, if Pierre agreed with Sam's assessment. John knew he'd certainly rather be in the Sharper Security prison than locked in some hot rat-infested hole run by Policía La Raza.

Pierre sounded resigned, "Edmond does not know ze ways of ze world yet. For him, it is all easy solutions. Quel désastre."

"Solutions can be found, but they are rarely easy. I have some business in La Raza Council already. Edmond may become part of that."

"Merde! Don't hurt him Sam. If you find him, Agence de Sécurité will have our own trial." Growing up the son of a tribal judge, John had a good enough understanding of the legal process to know that not only would Agence de Sécurité have their own trial of Edmond to decide if they would turn him over to Sharper Security, but that the result of that trial would ensure a third-party court would get involved.

"I understand, Pierre. I'll let you know."

Sam hung up the connection to Pierre and turned to face John, "Now we know what we're up against. At least it sounds like Pierre is going to let this play out legally."

John thought that despite sovereignty in representing its customers, Sharper Security sure seemed to spend a lot of time in legal wrangling. "What do you need me to do? You *are* planning a trip to La Raza Council, aren't you? I want to go."

Sam smiled, "Of course. We should be able to kill two birds with one stone and save resources all around. You're going in the truck with Raoul. If anything goes wrong with Policía La Raza, just keep him safe and get out if possible. Surrender if you can't get out and I'll work a trade of some sort. Let's meet Raoul in the garage and I'll show you."

Raoul followed the spider-like robot guide as it led him to the cavernous garage underneath the Sharper Security Prison. Sam's payment offer for helping deliver the Policía La Raza bandits back home was very generous. Enough gold that Raoul would be able to put quite a bit away for his retirement, or pay for his children's education, or buy that boat he'd always wanted. He knew in reality his wife would have something to say about what to do with the unexpected windfall, but for now, he could dream about what to spend it on.

Besides, he did feel sorry for the men who'd taken over his truck. They deserved some punishment, but he didn't think Pedro deserved to have his family taken away from him.

Raoul was admiring the vehicles in the garage when Sam and John arrived. He pointed at the Corvette, "Nice set of wheels. I admire your taste."

Sam grinned, "That's my favorite, but for this mission we need something with a little more passenger room, something a little more subtle." He gestured towards the plain white semi-truck and trailer parked along the east wall of the garage, "What do you think of that truck there?"

Raoul shook his head, "Looks solid enough, but isn't a truck like that designed for cargo? Two or three of us can ride in the cab of the tractor, but where will you put the prisoners? Locked in the back?"

"Let me show you." Sam led Raoul and John to the back of the 18 wheel truck's long trailer. He unlocked a small electronic lock with a key fob and opened the back doors to display a dull black metal wall. "Not all is as it seems. Step back." Sam triggered another button on the key fob and the top of the black metal wall toppled to the concrete floor with a loud crash, forming a ramp into the back of the truck. Solid metal hinges were revealed at the bottom. It was apparent that the eight-inch thick ramp would double very effectively as armor when raised.

"Madre de Dios!" Raoul gasped. "That is no ordinary truck." He peered into the back and noticed similar eight-inch armor protected the walls and floor, which along with the equipment embedded in the walls made the inside much smaller than expected.

"Come inside, I'll show you around. After all, you and John will need to know how to operate everything." Sam handed John the key fob as he led them up the ramp, "I can control everything remotely with the encrypted communications gear in my smart glasses, but you'll need this electronic key if you're going to be in charge of the truck."

"Aren't you coming with us? What if I lose them?" John asked a practical question, looking around inside the truck.

"I can reprogram the truck to no longer respond to the set of encryption keys stored inside the key fob in an instant." Sam replied, "First take a look inside. You can drive from back here, with a complete set of controls up front duplicating those in the cab. The cab is bullet-proof, but not as armored as back here. There is a locking passageway also from the cab to the back, so no need to drop the ramp unless you're moving something quickly or large." He gestured to the control stations and electronics inside the back of the truck.

John looked around, impressed by the inside of a truck that looked more like the inside of a fighting vehicle, "Those are targeting displays and radar?"

"Ground and air radar and targeting for not only the missile batteries embedded within the roof but for the camera aimed machine guns ready to fire from ports that open up along all sides.

Raoul thought for a second, "And the wheels?"

"Retractable armor can drop down to protect them, but they are a solid design that won't go flat. Besides, with eighteen wheels, even if one became a little uneven, you're still going to be able to drive out of most places." Sam smiled. "I wouldn't take it up against a modern tank, because even with some decent missile firepower, the truck's armor has too many right-angles to defeat a really big projectile launcher, but anything short of that will receive quite a surprise. Close the back up and I'll show you something else retractable."

As John pushed the button that slowly turned the ramp back into rear armor, lights came on within the back of the truck. Raoul thought he was taking the revelation of a fortress within a plain-looking truck trailer quite well.

Sam led them to what looked like a set of low seats running lengthwise down the center-middle of the trailer. The dozen seats had a solid rectangular base with black padding on the bottom and for the back. Half faced one side of the truck, the other half behind them the other side. "These seats are fairly comfortable, but they serve another purpose as well."

Sam unlocked something on the end of the row of seats and slid them apart, revealing a now open box beneath. "You can store things in here you don't want someone to find, but it's even more useful as a covert way out of the trailer." Sam triggered another release and the middle of the box bottom split in half, falling open to the ground below the trailer.

There is no end to the surprises of this truck, Raoul thought.

John was beginning to get the idea, "What about Pedro and his men?"

"They can sit in the seats back here while you lock them in. It won't be the most comfortable ride, but I'll be suited up and in the box before you bring them in. They can't know I'm with you. Let them assume I'm still back at the prison. Not only will that help deter an attack by Garcia, but they won't notice when I go my own way out the bottom." Sam closed up the bottom and then the top of the seat box with another electronic command. "Come on, I'll show you how to get out through the cab."

Raoul was feeling a lot safer about the whole trip as Sam showed them the passage to the cab and the protection measures built into it.

John still looked a little nervous as they climbed down from the cab and back out into the garage, "So I will be negotiating for Sharper Security? Leading Raoul in delivering Pedro and his men?"

Sam cuffed John on the back of the shoulders, "You'll be fine. We need you to talk to the Policía La Raza guards, but you'll have Raoul and Pedro with you and I'll be nearby. Let me handle any negotiation with Garcia. He can wonder why I'm audio-only, but he'll have to assume I'm staying out of reach."

Raoul thought John looked a little more confident, but not much. "I will drive this magnificent vehicle for you. There is nothing to worry about. We go, drop off the soldiers, pick up the gold and come home. What could be easier? Easier than facing my wife if I come home without my share of the gold."

"I suppose." John looked thoughtful.

"Let's go pick out some suitable equipment from the armory. I've wanted to give one of those stealth powered warrior suits some exercise anyway. Then you can go grab the prisoners while I try to make myself comfortable in that box."

Old I-10 Freeway, La Raza Council Border

Late afternoon

Edmond drove down the wide toll road, his car's Agence de Sécurité transponder ensuring quick passage. He'd never been to La Raza Council, but he knew they had no love for Sam Harper. Most places he could go, they'd arrest him as a fugitive and give him up if Sam requested it under an extradition agreement, but Policía La Raza only played by the rules when they wanted to. When it was in their interest, they could be counted on to conveniently ignore them, or at least come up with some excuse to do what they wanted. Besides, Edmond wasn't even sure La Raza Council had signed any of the more common extradition agreements. He knew they'd never given Agence de Sécurité any wanted prisoners.

A simple plan, Edmond thought. He'd been following Lieutenant Garcia's conversations with his father, Pierre. Policía La Raza wanted Shortee back. Sam wanted Edmond, so Garcia would think to trade Edmond for Shortee. Edmond knew Sam better than that, though. He'd watched his father's dealings with Sam over the years. Sam would never trade Shortee for anyone, now that he'd committed to holding him. That would leave Edmond in comfort under Policía La Raza's protection, able to plot his next move while Garcia kept him around to use as a bargaining chip with Sam.

Edmond thought he might even convince Garcia to give him some help in whatever his next move turned out to be. The enemy of my enemy is my friend, after all.

Arriving in his black Camaro at the La Raza Council border station, Edmond wondered why the northbound side of the toll road seemed to have a much heavier guard than the southbound side he was on. Both sides featured guard booths for protection from the sand and wind and a short line of cars and trucks approaching them. Maybe the northbound side was leftover from immigration checkpoints before the Big Split and thus needed to be larger.

A Policía La Raza soldier carrying an AK-47 style assault rifle on a sling approached his vehicle, "Identification and traveler's permit, please."

Edmond wasn't sure what to provide, Agence de Sécurité didn't use any paper forms, "Electronic identification?"

"You don't have any papers from La Raza Council, Señor?" The guard seemed skeptical. "Not many come to our border without making arrangements with the Council. A permit is needed to cross our land, even on the toll road. What is your business in La Raza Council?"

Edmond tried a weak smile, "If you will let Lieutenant Garcia of Policía La Raza know that Edmond, from Agence de Sécurité is here at the border, I think you will find that he wishes to see me."

"I will check, Señor. Remain in your vehicle."

Edmond watched as the soldier went to confer with his sergeant at a central guard post. The sergeant listened, and then seemed to confer electronically with someone else. In short order, he followed the soldier back to Edmond's car.

As Edmond turned to smile at the sergeant, he noticed the soldier's now fierce expression. The sergeant spoke first, while aiming a pistol at Edmond from a range too short to miss, "You will step out of the auto and come with us. El Teniente Garcia will be pleasured to speak to you. How much pleasure you find it, we shall see."

Edmond looked around and noticed that the soldier also had his longer weapon aimed directly at him from the passenger side of the car. Best to do what they said for now and sort this all out with Garcia.

Sam bounced around a little as the truck hit some sort of defect in the road. The exoskeleton and armor stealth suit from MIT he was wearing absorbed most of the shock of the semi-truck and trailer on the road, but that didn't make lying on his back in a box for over an hour comfortable. Besides, most of the shock absorption in the suit was designed to reduce shock in the arms and legs, not this relatively slow bouncing up and down on his back.

The heads-up-display (HUD) in the suit's visor kept his mind occupied. Kept his mind away from the threat of claustrophobia from the confined space he traveled in. Sam's ability to watch and listen to the various microphone and camera feeds inside and outside the truck helped, as did his ability to communicate back to the Sharper Security expert systems without a noticeable time delay. Their processing power in turn enabled him to notice and identify many things he'd otherwise miss if he had to monitor all the cameras and microphones himself.

Up above, Raoul was driving the truck from the cab, looking like an ordinary trucker. John was in the trailer, sitting with the prisoners. The prisoners strapped in with their butts located a few inches above Sam's head. He tried not to think about it and focus instead on watching them in his visor from a more enjoyable angle.

John sat at a control console facing the prisoners and talked with Pedro, who seemed to be the only one of his men to speak English well, or at least who would admit to it. "We are almost to the border station on I-10. We still have another hour's drive to the Policía La Raza headquarters, but you'll be home soon."

Pedro grunted, "Home. Yes, perhaps."

Sam typed by forming his suited fingers into various combinations that the wearable computer inside the suit interpreted as letters. So close to the prisoners, he didn't want to risk speaking above a whisper. Not even that, as long as he had an alternative available. It did slow down his outgoing communications, though.

As Raoul drove, Sam watched the road ahead in one half of his visor and continued to keep his other eye on John and the prisoners above in the other half. Normally he'd only use a small portion of the visor with a transparency setting, but currently there was nothing else to see except the inside of the box confining him.

"Why do you follow La Raza Council? There are many other sovereignties you can subscribe to. I know they are cheap for poor people, with progressive rates, but it seems to me that they don't run things in the best interests of their clients. They act more like a government from before the Big Split, don't they? Telling you what to do all the time?" John seemed genuinely curious.

"My family has lived near Tucson for a hundred years. After the Big Split, the old Tucson City Council took over the area, called it La Raza Council instead. They promised that those who followed them would never go hungry. That we would never have our land taken away. Told us we would not be enslaved by the Norte Americanos. My family believed them. Mi familia es todo para mi." Now that Pedro was almost home, he'd suddenly become much more talkative.

John glanced down at the console in front of him to check the perimeter of the area they traveled through, and then looked at Pedro again, "Do *you* believe them? You've seen at least part of the Arizona Zone outside La Raza Council. You know a little of what it's like."

Sam admired John's persistence, but wasn't sure he was going to get through to Pedro. The brainwashing that went on in La Raza run schools and society was a hard thing to get past.

Pedro engaged, "I watched from the black ridge as your people did the things that people do. I know that the rich people near your prison live well, but I am sure you have the oppressed and poor among you somewhere. Your rich don't live much better than our Council Members."

John couldn't help but laugh, "The people who live near the prison are some of the poorest, living outside of town because the land is less expensive. Who would want to live near a prison? Most of the rich people Sharper Security protects live within Maricopa City. Even the poorest Pima on the reservation lives almost as nicely as the people you saw near the prison."

Pedro looked puzzled, "But they all had their own land. Acres of land, with walls and fences. Large homes, not old run down apartments. How can they be poor?"

John thought for a second, "Have you seen pictures of Tucson from before the Big Split?" After a moment of playing with the controls on his console, John projected some video up on the wall of the truck interior. "This is downtown Tucson from twenty years ago, before it was ruined." The video changed to a swath of destruction, with destroyed buildings and rubble everywhere, "This is Phoenix from fifteen years ago, right after the Big Split, when they bombed the place." He switched the video to a view of towering skyscrapers in the desert, "This is Phoenix right now, risen from the ashes of that attack. How does that compare to Tucson, which was only ruined by rioting?"

Pedro was stunned. His men watched the video curiously, but they apparently weren't following the conversation.

John continued, showing an overhead view of Maricopa City, "This is a live view of Maricopa from a Sharper Security aerial drone. These homes are mostly older, from before the Big Split, but they've been well taken care of and the edges of town have grown a lot since I was a child on the reservation. See the people, the stores, and the cars. To you they must all seem rich, but they are normal people. Retired people, people who don't want to live in a big city. How can there be that many *rich* people?"

Pedro thought for a while. "Not many in La Raza Council have access, but they say the pictures we see online are lies. Tales from before the wars, meant to fool people." Sam decided he might just believe the evidence in front of his eyes with a little more prodding.

John had already anticipated this, "Watch the video." He said, as he directed the drone flying over Maricopa City west away from town. It was obvious even to Pedro that the view was one camera shot with no tricks as it reached the area around the prison. "I said this was a live video. Do you recognize the area? Looks just like you just saw it yourself, right? If we had time, I'd take you into the city and you could see the rest for yourself. The world is a much bigger place than La Raza Council wants you to believe."

Pedro was silent, thinking for a few minutes.

Sam felt another bounce in the road and decided he needed to consider an upgrade to the semi-truck and trailer's suspension system. The air-conditioning built into the suit would just heat up the air of the compartment Sam had stashed himself in, so he was thankful for the slight breeze from the compartment's vent. Even so, sweat formed on his forehead as his body heat and the electronics of the suit combined with the hot air from outside to slowly raise the temperature in the box. He estimated he'd be able to leave before cooking to death, but that didn't make it more comfortable, nor make him stop hoping Raoul and John would hurry up to their destination.

John made his pitch as only one newly converted can, "You say your family is the most important thing to you. Why not sign them up with Sharper Security to protect them? Leave La Raza Council. They won't be able to harm you; Sam will make sure of that. Then you can live with some freedom, with the ability to work for yourself, not for the Garcias of the world."

Sam starting sending a message with his fingers, mentally cursing John's enthusiasm. While he sympathized with the people of La Raza Council, this wasn't exactly an ideal time to get into an open fight with Policía La Raza. Tensions were high enough already, trying to capture Edmond without hurting him, while still holding on to Shortee Tejada. Adding Pedro's whole family to the mix was definitely not part of the plan.

"I will do it." Pedro said, surprisingly decisive. "From now on, Sam Harper es mi Patron and as head of the Guerrera family, I sign mi familia up also. There is mi esposa, our three daughters and mijo. Look, I have pictures I carry with me always. Also, there is mi suegra, my mother-in-law, who lives with us. What do I need to do so as to sign up?"

John looked pleased as he released Pedro's restraints, "Come over to the console. I've found some standard paperwork Sam uses. I'll need everyone's name. A copy of those photos is helpful as well."

Sam sighed and deleted his half formed text message to John, and then started another. He hadn't been completely sure he could keep John and Raoul safe while grabbing Edmond. How was he going to get Pedro and his family out?

Pedro finished signing the paperwork electronically, and then turned to his former soldiers in Policía La Raza, "You are all young and single, but how many of you want to sign on with Sharper Security with me? The rest of you must not say a thing, or I will find you and I will cut you. You understand?"

With that recruiting pitch, all of Pedro's soldiers decided they wanted to sign-up as well, so John released them from their restraints. Lying on his back under the rear-ends of his new clients, Sam Harper sighed again.

Rita Road, South Tucson, La Raza Council

About that same time

Garcia smiled at the knock on his office door, turning his chair away from the window. He'd watched Sanchez and Diaz on video, the two soldiers escorting Edmond, as they approached with their prisoner. He sat up in his chair and tossed his latest beer can into the recycling bin, "Entra."

Sanchez and Diaz entered, pushing Edmond between them. Sanchez saluted, "Corporal Sanchez reporting with the prisoner, El Teniente Garcia." Diaz lay Edmond's weapons and communications gear on Garcia's desk.

Garcia nodded, swept Edmond's things into a drawer, and then reached under his desk where he kept his own pistol, just in case, "Remove his restraints, but stay just outside the door. I will speak with him here."

Sanchez released Edmond, and then followed Diaz out the door. Even though Garcia was a bit on the rotund side and the prisoner was young and lean, the two soldiers weren't worried about el teniente. Garcia preferred to be feared by his men. He didn't coddle them.

Garcia watched Edmond rub his wrists where the restraints had been, waiting for his prisoner to speak. He was just a kid, barely eighteen. Easy to break.

Edmond started by trying to bargain, "Lieutenant Garcia, I can help you get Shortee Tejada back from Sharper Security."

"You are the one who arrested him. If you had brought him to me instead, we could have worked something out. Instead, he is in that gabacho's prison. I am not sure you are in a position to help yourself, let alone help me with anything." Best to show him who was in charge right away, Garcia thought.

Not put off, Edmond took a step closer to Garcia's desk. "I am wanted by Sam Harper for a misunderstanding with one of his clients. He may trade Shortee to you in exchange for me."

"A misunderstanding?" Garcia was interested in what Edmond was caught up in. Something muy mal, to make him flee to La Raza Council after arresting the son of a prominent political family.

"A woman he is protecting. She killed my parents. I have nothing against Sam directly, but his interests aren't mine." Garcia was sure there was more to the story than that.

"And your father, Pierre? He will not stand for you?" Garcia was still a little leery about potentially starting a war with Sharper Security and Agence de Sécurité simultaneously.

Edmond looked down, "He must do what is best for Agence de Sécurité. I fight my own battles." Edmond turned to peer out the window behind Garcia's desk. "You have a nice view."

Garcia continued to watch Edmond. He knew what the view outside his own window looked like. "You brought a vehicle owned by Agence de Sécurité. A black Camaro. It has communications equipment in it, keyed to your biometrics. You will unlock it and give me the encryption codes for your Agence. That will pay for your protection here against Sharper Security."

Edmond looked shocked now, "I came to you voluntarily. To help you get Shortee Tejada back from Sharper Security. You expect me to betray my father?"

Garcia shrugged, "I expect you to realize that you are now completely within my power. Whether you live or die is up to me. I will be muy triste, very sad, when I explain to Pierre how you were killed by a gang while trying to purchase illegal weapons." Garcia raised his voice, "Guards. Come take this one to the cellar.", then lowered it again, "Not many buildings here have a cellar. You will not find our cellar very pleasant."

As Sanchez and Diaz re-entered the room, Edmond took another step towards Garcia, "You can't do this!" he protested.

In that moment, Garcia produced a silver steel pistol from beneath his desk and pointed it at Edmond's face, "Oh yes, yes I can. You will have some time to think before our next interview. I will have some time to think of your penalty for arresting Shortee in the first place and dumping this mess into my lap. Now put the restraints back on and sé un niño bueno." *Be a good boy.*

Sanchez replaced the restraints on Edmond while Diaz held him in place. Each of the two soldiers grabbed an arm to march Edmond out the door.

"I will have my revenge!" Edmond shouted as they led him out the door.

Garcia wasn't sure if he meant his revenge against the women Sam was protecting, or against him. Garcia shrugged again. No matter, he doubted either would occur. Best to let him realize his true situation and then discuss his options again.

In the meantime, he would message Sam Harper and see if he was interested in a trade. Despite his possible profit from holding Edmond, getting Shortee Tejada back was still his immediate problem. Hmm.... Sam's associates were coming soon to exchange prisoners for gold. Perhaps there was an opportunity there for a package deal, Edmond and his associates for Shortee. Or perhaps drawing Sam where Policía La Raza would have an advantage. It bore thinking about.

Old I-10 Freeway, La Raza Council Border

About that same time

Raoul watched the Policía La Raza soldiers at the border checkpoint as he drove Sam's disguised truck closer. He'd been through the checkpoint before several times, but never with a load of armored military hardware in the back. As he slowed to a stop in the line for commercial vehicles, he felt John climb into the cab from the back.

"I will speak to them." Raoul said and rolled down the driver-side window.

John and Raoul watched a soldier approach as the truck reached the front of the line next to one of the border station guard booths.

"Identification and cargo permit, please." The AK-47 style assault rifle carrying soldier demanded.

Raoul smiled as he handed over a paper, "Here is my La Raza Council identification card. I drive here frequently. No cargo permit today. I carry passengers to Policía Lieutenant Garcia."

The soldier frowned, "He is popular today. I will see what this is about." He took the identification paper and walked back to the sergeant supervising the border checkpoint.

John and Raoul watched them talk, and then watched the sergeant communicate with someone they couldn't see. Raoul was a little nervous when he sent the soldier to gather more soldiers from the nearby booths. He was *very* nervous when those same soldiers spread out and surrounded the truck. Madre de Dios! Would he forever be in danger this week?

"I'd better speak with him." John sounded much calmer than Raoul felt.

The sergeant of the guard approached the open driver-side window, "You will step out of the truck and we will inspect your passengers."

John leaned over to the window, "I am with Sharper Security. My orders are to deliver the prisoners only to Garcia at your headquarters on Rita Road. Tell Garcia that if he wishes, we will turn and go, but under our contract with Policía La Raza, he will forfeit the amount of the payment if he refuses delivery of the prisoners."

Raoul wasn't sure John's aggressive manner was the best position to take when surrounded by soldiers with automatic weapons.

The sergeant didn't seem pleased, but did seem to be listening to someone in his ear. "El Teniente instructs me. You may proceed, but we will send an escort to lead you to the right place. We would not want you to become lost while in La Raza Council."

"Thank you. I knew we could straighten this out." John replied.

The sergeant smiled wolfishly and then directed some of the soldiers to a pair of older tan SUVs with Policía La Raza markings, "You will follow the front vehicle and not lose the rear one. You will not deviate from the course. If you have a problem, you will stop and they will stop with you and investigate. Do you have any questions about the procedure you will follow?"

Raoul shook his head as he moved the truck back into gear, "No, sergeant. It will be just as you say."

Hidden Valley Road, Maricopa, Arizona Zone

About that same time

Evie rolled over on to her right side in the prison infirmary bed and watched a robot clean up the room on the other side of the glass partition. She wondered where John and Sam were. The Sharper Services EMT had just left, taking a blood sample with him and giving assurances she'd be allowed back out of bed by the next day at the latest.

She was still in shock after that sniper attack, she decided. The pain in her left side was gone, but she felt sore all over. She thought about her ruined home. Felt her breath go short, then a sob. She decided she hated Arizona Zone as the water droplets began to stream from the outside corners of her eyes. Each sob brought pain back to her side.

Why her? What had she done to deserve all this? None of this would have happened if Hamish hadn't left her. Why didn't he just run with the rest of his men? She knew his work was dangerous. She'd always dreaded a knock in the middle of the night whenever he was on an extended assignment, but she'd never expected anything to actually happen to him. She'd always been more afraid for herself, even though she'd mostly held a succession of desk jobs, not really getting back into the field after her work in Paris.

As her sobs slowed down, Evie looked around for a nurse, or a call button. She could really use a drink right about now. What kind of service did they have in this prison hospital, anyway?

Rita Road, South Tucson, La Raza Council

Dusk

Edmond was marched between the two soldiers, Sanchez and Diaz, down the short stone steps to the underground cellar. The soldiers led him into a small four foot square stone cell with a low ceiling. Edmond couldn't quite stand up straight inside the cell.

Closing the door made of steel bars behind him and locking it with a small key, Sanchez ordered him to strip and pass all of his possessions out through the bars. "The trustee will have new clothes for you." Diaz added.

Upstairs, Sanchez and Diaz had taken a few minutes to thoroughly beat him in the Guard corporal's office. With batons at first, and then with their fists and boots. He wasn't sure if the beating was for protesting to Garcia, or just general policy for new prisoners. Edmond just knew they seemed to have a lot of experience, using well-practiced motions to hit him repeatedly on large muscle groups. Muscles where it would hurt, but not do much permanent damage.

His gut, Edmond decided. His gut hurt the most. His leg and arm muscles were in contention, but his gut won. Maybe his shoulder blades. They were hard to rub and even harder to protect from the soldier's repeated strikes. Still, there was something lasting about the pain in his gut. Maybe some internal bleeding or a ruptured organ. He was proud of the fact that he hadn't cried out, hadn't shed a tear, hadn't even whimpered a little.

The two soldiers seemed to take pleasure in their work, Sanchez especially, but not to have any particular objective. He supposed their orders were to take him back to Garcia later, not interrogate him themselves.

Edmond groaned as he slowly finished removing his last article of clothing and passed it through the bars. He hadn't brought much into the building with him and he'd left his Camaro locked. Edmond knew they'd have to break into it if they wanted to get in. He wasn't sure they wouldn't break him first.

Sanchez took Edmond's clothing and other possessions and walked down to the other end of the corridor, away from the entrance steps. Garcia tossed a bar of soap into Edmond's cell and turned on what looked like a large garden hose, pushing the nozzle through the top of the bars and then clamping it into place before turning away. This looked like a familiar routine for the two soldiers.

There was no place in the cell to avoid the cold water streaming in, just a drain in the middle so water didn't build up and spill out into the corridor between the cells. Hot outside the building, Edmond shivered inside the cold stone and even colder water.

The cold at least it seemed to make his new bruises hurt a little less. His relief was short. He began to shiver.

Minutes passed and the guards didn't return. Edmond felt himself turning blue, huddling naked against one rough stone wall, trying to stay as warm as possible. Trying to rub his bruises and create a little heat at the same time.

Edmond reached up to grasp the silver cross he usually wore around his neck, and then remembered it had been taken with the rest of his things. He considered trying to knock the hose nozzle down from the top of the bars, but survival instincts warned him that Sanchez might use that as an excuse for another beating.

Finally, several more minutes later, the water stopped. Edmond could breathe again. A well fed, but muscular man in grey clothing with broad red stripes came by the door of the cell and unhooked the hose. "You are new here. Understand that here is my law. You do what I tell you. We all do what the guards tell us. Maybe you survive, maybe you do not survive. Here is some clothing. You will not get more." The trustee tossed a grey set of pants and shirt into the cell next to Edmond.

"Underwear?" Edmond asked. "Is there a bathroom?"

The trustee laughed, "You will make do. You have a drain." He shook his head as he walked off, "Underwear!" he said under his breath.

The clothing was scratchy, but warmer than sitting naked on a stone floor. He found that sitting with his legs out, back leaning up against the stone wall, was the most comfortable position. His father was right. For the hundredth time in the last hour, he wished he was back home.

Edmond could make out more cells across the way and down the corridor outside, but he didn't want to call any attention to himself by trying to communicate with the other prisoners. Better to wait and see who they were. He groaned again, feeling his painful muscles.

Sam Harper lay on his back watching video feeds in the visor of his warrior suit. He'd watched as they passed through the heart of Tucson on I-10 and then took the freeway off-ramp to head South on Rita Road. Now, as the tan SUV leading them approached the entrance to the fenced Policia La Raza complex on the east side of the road, he knew he needed to separate from John and Raoul soon.

The lead vehicle didn't worry him, but the trailing tan SUV did. They'd be watching the truck and might notice a fighting suit depart from it. For once, luck was with him. The lead vehicle passed up the first driveway into the 1000 foot square complex and led them to the second entrance. The trail vehicle turned into the first driveway, closer to their barracks, apparently satisfied that their work was done.

Sloppy, but helpful, Sam thought. As the lead tan SUV turned left into the driveway and stopped at the gate, the Raoul naturally stopped the truck on the road behind, apparently waiting to turn into the driveway once the gate was open. In the process, he blocked any view of the west side of the truck from the Policia La Raza complex. The truck was tall enough that not even the guard towers in the corners and center of the fenced area could see most of the other side.

Sam's GPS read 32.07202,-110.80703. Time to go. He lifted himself on bent arms and feet, and then activated the floor mechanism with a signal from his wearable computer. The bottom of the box opened itself. A relief, after spending the last couple of hours cooped inside.

Dropping to the ground, the impact on his limbs was absorbed by the exoskeleton in the suit he wore. Quickly, he rolled west, out from under the truck and across the other side of the road. He continued rolling over a sandy drop-off from the edge of the road and then crawled behind a tall, handy creosote bush. He didn't think he'd been seen.

Sam watched the truck start moving again and turn into the driveway, following the tan SUV through the gate. About 30 feet from the chain-link fence was a tall earthen berm. The berm had obviously been there for years, with vertical drainage lines from infrequent rains marring its surface. The truck passed through an opening in the berm and passed out of sight.

"You still rolling around in the dirt back there?" John asked in Sam's ear. Obviously, he'd been watching Sam leave the truck.

"It'll be dark soon. Try not to get yourselves killed before then and I'll see what I can do about joining you inside the wire. Oh, and tell Raoul to park the truck where he won't have to back up in order to make a run at one of the gaps in that berm. You may need to leave in a hurry." Sam thought John should've already thought of that, but no harm in reminding him. "Always plan your retreat before the fight starts so that you don't have to waste time thinking about escape when it's time to leave. That's lesson number four."

"Anything you want me to tell Garcia?" John asked.

"What I have to say to him might get him a bit upset at you. Better let me talk to him over the radio when he shows up. That'll help convince him I'm still up north." Sam thought John would be able to handle Garcia in a discussion, but he also knew Garcia would be heavier-handed with someone standing in the middle of his headquarters than with someone he couldn't reach directly.

Sam turned off the audio and concentrated on his own upcoming trip into the complex. He wasn't sure he could avoid setting off an alarm, but he didn't want to leave any evidence that it was anything other than a false alarm. Certainly, they must get plenty of those out in the desert, from stray dogs or coyotes, or even birds landing where they weren't expected.

A cut fence or something seen by a soldier's own eyes would be impossible to dismiss as a false alarm. If he could enter while only tripping the electronic sensors sure to be in place around the perimeter, that was easier to explain away by a lazy soldier intent on not working too hard.

Sam guessed that the chain-link fence with razor wire on top likely had sensors, both in the fence and in the ground beneath. The perimeter berm might also have some sort of detection system. Farther inside the complex, it was likely that only doors and windows had anything connected to a sensor; otherwise, the personnel going about their regular business would set them off with no benefit to those on guard detail.

Pedro was worried. Worried about his mother, his wife and his four children. Three young girls, then finally a baby boy. Pedro expected he might eventually have a few more children, if his family made it out of this situation alive.

John seemed like a good man and Pedro knew Sam's reputation, even in La Raza Council. Sam always seemed to come out on top in the minor run ins Policía La Raza experienced with Sharper Security in the past. Still, Pedro was worried.

When the truck stopped, John released Pedro and brought him into the cab of the truck to see the headquarters complex. "It is just as you described it." John said.

"It was my home away from home. I have spent many nights in those wooden barracks on the north side, past the firing range." Pedro was suddenly homesick for his wife. He pointed, "My family should be in the cellar of that stone building."

John nodded, a little less sure of himself now that they were in the middle of the enemy complex, "Sam will get them out, or die trying."

Pedro wasn't impressed by the way John described Sharper Security's plan, "It will do mi familia no good for Sam to die trying. Mi familia es todo para mi."

Raoul spoke up from the other side of the cab, "You hijacked my truck, but if anyone can get them out, Sam will, and I hope he does."

Pedro nodded, "I am sorry. I was following Garcia's orders, but you did not deserve to become involved."

John pointed to a rotund Policía La Raza lieutenant exiting the headquarters building, "Looks like Garcia's coming to inspect the merchandise." He tossed a key fob to Pedro, "Here, go get your men ready to come out through the cab."

"Mi familia es todo para mi." Pedro repeated. "I will prepare my soldiers for what is needed."

Sam called Garcia, routing the audio through his office up north and leaving the video for the call blank. Still concealed behind a tall creosote bush across the road, he watched Garcia approaching the truck via a video feed. "The truck with the prisoners has arrived, but you won't get them until my men see the gold."

Garcia stopped walking in the video feed, "I have the gold ready. I want to see the prisoners."

"As a gesture of good faith, my men have brought them to your headquarters complex. They won't let anyone depart the truck until they see the gold through the windows. We wouldn't want there to be any misunderstanding about delivery, would we?" Sam didn't trust Garcia to tie a little kid's shoes without looking for an angle to take advantage of him.

Garcia paused for a moment before replying, "I will bring out the gold shortly. Your men had better be ready to bring out the prisoners."

Sam wasn't convinced Garcia even had the gold ready, but that fit his plans just fine, "Call me when you have the gold where they can see it. It's comfortable in the cab of that truck, designed for long drives. They aren't going anywhere."

"We will talk again soon." Garcia replied before disconnecting the call and walking back into the stone headquarters building.

Perfect timing, Sam thought. Just getting dark enough that a black stealth suit wasn't going to be noticed in the shadows of a building. He called John and made sure he'd heard the conversation with Garcia, and then stood up behind the tall creosote bush. No time like the present.

Sam started running across the road, through the dirt on the other side and toward the chain-link fence surrounding the complex. The augmented muscles in his suit pushed his acceleration faster than a world-champion sprinter, while requiring much less effort.

The top of a boulder poked out of the sandy soil near the fence. That was his target. Stepping on the boulder in full stride, Sam jumped with most of the power of the suit's exoskeleton augmented muscles.

Flinging himself through the air like a long jumper, he cleared the ten foot chain-link fence at a fifty degree angle. Sam hit the top of his arc over halfway between the fence and the dirt berm. He landed just over the top of the berm, sliding down the far side with a scraping noise. The exoskeleton legs absorbed most of the impact.

Sam leapt to his feet. He began sprinting again. If he'd triggered an alarm, he didn't want to still be here when someone came to check it out. He had seconds.

Adrenaline pumping. Sam ran full speed through the shadows of a barracks building. Soldiers would be settling in for the night. Across a parking lot. Policía La Raza vehicles that all looked the same. He could see the Sharper Security truck across the lot. Parked out of the way, facing the north driveway.

Past a building marked armory. Sam made a mental note. Through the open firing range. Sticking close to the shadows of its backstops.

Finally, across an old asphalt path. A three story stone building ahead coming in a blur. Sam jumped again. This time, forty feet, almost straight up. Landed on the roof.

Found the part of the building above where Pedro had placed Garcia's office. Climbed down over the edge. Used an arm and a leg to lock himself into place under the shadows of the eaves. Looked in the window. The office was dark.

Sam waited for the alarm.

Garcia stood in the ground floor hallway, directing his men to their positions. He spoke to the Sergeant of the Guard at his unit's barracks building over a headset while simultaneously pointing soldiers passing around him to the positions he wanted them in.

Overwatch from the rooftops, check. Small squads directed to take up positions near the firing range and behind walls, check. Garcia knew he should have positioned most of them earlier, but he wasn't even sure the Sharper Security truck with the returning prisoners would make it all the way in, let alone just park in the middle of Policía La Raza headquarters and no one get out.

He knew Sam well enough to believe he wouldn't lie about the prisoners being in the nondescript truck, but what else was in there? Better to not take a risk. Better to surround them and ensure no one did anything without his knowledge. Stay in control of the situation, Garcia thought.

The silent alarm notification came as a surprise. A motion sensor tripped on one of the north perimeter berms. Nothing from the fences, though. Perhaps the truck released a surveillance robot? Garcia sighed and let the men in the guard towers know to start scanning the inside of the perimeter. He then divided men from the stone headquarters building into a couple of teams, diverting them to become search parties to cover the grounds and look for anything out of place. The search left Garcia feeling spread a little thin, and the clerks were going to scream later about being turned into foot soldiers, but he wasn't about to let Sam's men get away with anything on his turf.

All the dispositions he needed made for now, Garcia headed to an elevator. Time to go back to his office and check on the status of that gold shipment. With La Raza Council's internal currency only accepted at a severe discount by non-council subscribers, most payments to outsiders had to be in gold or another hard currency. That made it hard to come by, but Garcia had called in yet another set of favors.

At the end of this, Councilmember Tejada had better be grateful, Garcia thought. If not, Garcia had called in so many favors he wasn't going to have enough power to get a good table at a restaurant. For now, he was sweating and could really use a cold beer from the fridge in his office.

Sam watched silently through a thermal imaging overlay in his suit's visor as Policía La Raza soldiers finished taking up positions to guard the truck and sweep the perimeter. Sam saw a pair of squads take a special interest in the part of the berm he'd traversed. Fortunately, none of them were familiar enough with the desert landscape to recognize as important the long and deep tracks he'd left in the dirt while sprinting into the center of the complex.

Satisfied that the alarm had already been given, albeit a silent alarm, and that the guards would be focused out on the grounds of the complex, Sam turned his attention to the third floor window next to him. A little augmented pressure in the right place and the window catch was ineffective to keep him from sliding the window carefully open. No visible security measures on the window itself, but who would be trying to sneak into a third floor window in the middle of Policía La Raza headquarters?

Sliding silently into the room, Sam made sure the window closed firmly behind him. A quick search of the room revealed Garcia's desk pistol. Sam quickly removed the striker from the Glock pistol and then replaced it in the desk holster. He also cut the wires to a panic button in the desk. No one would be closing that alarm circuit without a bit of repair work first. Sam settled down to wait in a corner opposite the window and near the door.

He didn't wait long. With Sam's hearing augmented by the suit helmet, he heard footsteps in the corridor outside, and then the door open into the office. He turned his head enough to watch as the portly Garcia entered the office, grabbed a beer from the fridge, and then settled into his chair, looking out the window.

With Garcia's back to him, Sam was sure he hadn't been seen. Not yet, anyway. He glided forward until he was within reach of Garcia's head. Listened carefully. Confident Garcia wasn't speaking, nor listening; Sam snatched the headset off his head and tossed it casually across the room.

Garcia spun around in his chair. His right hand darted for his desk pistol while his left stabbed the handy panic button.

Sam watched from behind his visor as Garcia spoke, "Who are you? What do you want?" He was probably trying to buy time for his men to arrive, estimating his pistol would not penetrate Sam's suit. Garcia's pupils dilated as he took in Sam's exoskeleton armor suit.

To reinforce the point he was about to make, Sam pointed the automatic weapon built-in to the right arm of his suit at Garcia's chest. "As usual, you are quite a bit outgunned. Be smart. Put the pistol down and stand up." Sam wasn't afraid of a pistol that wouldn't fire without a new way to trigger the primer. However, he preferred Garcia didn't realize his soldiers weren't coming. Waiting for them to arrive, he was likely to cooperate more while playing for time.

Garcia read the situation for a second, and then placed the Glock down on his desk, still within reach. "I recognize the voice behind the visor. Sam Harper?" As expected, Garcia took the expedient way out. The way Sam had left him, expecting the soldiers summoned by his alarm to rescue him later. Always let your enemy believe he still has a way out; that he isn't trapped yet. He'd have to mention that one to John later.

Sam nodded, "Now we're going to take a little walk. If I have to fight my way out, you're going to be the first casualty. It's getting on to night and you've got the whole place stirred up outside, so I don't anticipate running into many of your soldiers, but if we do, just remember to be convincing enough to keep yourself alive." Sam felt sure Garcia would realize it would be impossible for Sam to miss him from such short range.

Garcia looked Sam over again, and then conceded, "I may have to explain that suit, but other than being ten times as expensive as our nicest equipment, there aren't any markings on it to indicate it's not one of ours. I don't know how you think you're going to walk out of here, though. You won't be able to take me with you without making a lot of people suspicious."

Sam smiled under his visor, even though Garcia couldn't see it, "You let me worry about that. Let's start with a tour of wherever you're holding Edmond. He's a wanted fugitive and after I came all this way, I thought I'd take him off your hands."

"This way." is all Garcia commented. Sam could see that he felt beaten right now, but still held out hope for the situation to reverse itself in time.

Following Garcia through the door, Sam said "Let's take the stairs. Elevators are too easy for someone with a suspicious mind watching a security monitor to turn off. You don't mind the exercise, do you?"

"As long as we're going down the stairs and not up them." Garcia was still looking for an edge to turn the situation back around and was content to spar verbally in the meantime. Amazing how much better his English was in person.

Sam followed Garcia down the concrete stairwell to the ground floor. After a slight detour through a corridor, they stepped down short stone steps and into the cold cellar.

Garcia took care of the two guards at the cellar door while Sam casually covered them all, "Sanchez, give me your cell keys and go guard the front entrance outside with Diaz. We'll keep an eye on things down here."

Sanchez, with no inclination to question orders, handed over his set of keys and left with Diaz.

Edmond, back bent, leaned against the cold stone wall and scratched an itch where his grey clothing had rubbed his waist raw. He groaned and slowly moved his stiff and sore legs up and down to get a little more circulation.

Garcia arrived at the bars outside Edmond's four foot square cell. A tall man wearing a menacing black exoskeleton and armor suit followed just behind him. Edmond recognized the suit as a very expensive piece of equipment, but couldn't make out the face of the man behind the darkened helmet visor. Was the man here with Garcia to inflict more punishment somehow? To get the encryption key information out of him with more torture?

"Here he is." Garcia said as he pointed into Edmond's cell. "It would have been better for you to trade Shortee."

The man spoke from beneath the darkened visor, "I have a contract to keep Shortee as a prisoner. I gave my word, but I'm not sure you understand how that works. Keeping one's agreements. You probably never expected my men to make it out of La Raza Council alive with the payment for the prisoners."

Edmond felt hope rush into his chest. That sounded like Sam Harper. He'd take Sam's prison over the facilities here at Policia La Raza. "Sam?"

Sam nodded, "Edmond, you're under arrest for what you've been doing to Evie. I'm going to take you back with me."

"I'll come willingly." Edmond said. "The sooner the better."

Garcia didn't move to unlock the cell door, "You should surrender now and throw yourself on my mercy. Otherwise, you won't make it out of here alive."

Sam raised his visor so that Garcia could see his eyes, and then pointed the automatic weapon barrel attached to his right arm directly at Garcia's chest. "Whether we do or not, you have more immediate problems to worry about. Your guards may respond if I fill you with holes, but these stone walls are thick and I'm sure they've heard stranger sounds down here before. Are you sure you want to sacrifice your life to increase our odds of being caught a tiny bit more? I'm willing to take the chance."

Garcia unlocked the cell door. "This isn't the end of this." Garcia didn't sound very confident in his prediction. Edmond wished he'd been able to handle Garcia like that.

Edmond stepped out of the cell and stretched, reaching briefly for the ceiling. "My stuff. I need my clothing, my silver cross, the keys to my car, and my communications equipment."

Sam gestured down the corridor between the cells, "Garcia. Please lead the way to Edmond's things. Also, I'd like to see Pedro's family. I believe you have them here as well."

Garcia shook his head, "Edmond's possessions are upstairs in my office and I'm sure Pedro's family is safe at home right now, under protective guard."

How dare he lie like that? Edmond pointed down the corridor between the cells, away from the steps leading out of the cellar, "They took my possessions that way. No way that goes to Garcia's office."

Sam prodded Garcia down the corridor ahead of them, closing his helmet visor again, "I bet we'll also find some more visitors here. Fortunately," Sam tapped his visor with his left hand, "I took the precaution of bringing some photographs of the people I'm looking for. I hope they're in better shape than Edmond is. If not, I may ask you to return to Sharper Security prison as well, Garcia."

Garcia bowed his head and muttered something in Spanish about el diablo, but he led them down the corridor to where Edmond's things were stored in a drawer. While they walked, Sam seemed to be scanning the people in the cells, his head turning slightly left and right as they passed each group. The cells were sparsely populated because this was primarily used as a temporary holding space, but most of the inmates were quiet and broken looking in their grey clothing.

Sam picked up Edmond's car keys, "Edmond, grab your other things." He turned to Garcia, "I'm surprised you didn't say anything when we passed that larger cell with the older and younger women, three girls and a baby boy. It's almost like you weren't planning on pointing out Pedro's family to me."

Garcia faked a little surprise, "I don't know how they came to be here. Perhaps an overzealous subordinate. My men are always trying to anticipate my orders." Garcia shrugged.

Edmond grabbed his clothing first, awkwardly starting to slowly strip with an occasional wince of pain and soreness. Real underwear again!

Sam glanced at Edmond, and then gestured Garcia back down the corridor, "We'll go check on Pedro's family while you finish getting dressed. I'm sure you don't plan on staying here without me."

With a little more prodding, Garcia led Sam back down the long corridor to the larger cell containing Pedro's family. The cell was comfortable compared to most of the others, containing three metal-framed beds and a table with two chairs.

"Unlock it." Sam said. Edmond finished dressing and hurried after them as quickly as sore muscles would let him.

Garcia unlocked the door. Pedro's family crowded against the back wall, the two women in front of the three little girls, the younger woman holding a male baby.

Sam pulled a small wireless headset out of his left pocket and handed it to the younger woman. "Put it on. Someone would like to speak with you."

A little confused, she did as Sam said. Immediately, her face light up. "Pedro?" she said, followed by rapid Spanish Edmond had a hard time following. "Is ok." she said to Sam, handing the headset back. "We go with you."

Sam turned to Edmond, "Bring up the rear. Make sure no one is left behind." Sam gestured down the corridor towards the stairs up from the cellar, "Garcia, you've probably figured out by now that your guards aren't going to respond to that silent alarm you pressed in your office. Lead the way upstairs and outside. Remember, you'll be the first to pay for an attack on us."

John watched from the passenger seat in the cab of the truck as another tan Policia SUV arrived and soldiers brought out ten pounds of gold, a third of a gold bar. They set it visibly on a canvas bag at the entrance to the headquarters. The light from the outdoor fixtures near the entrance gleamed in reflection from the gold. John assumed it was the full ten pounds. After all, that's what Sam had bargained for. Looked about right, anyway. He glanced over at Raoul, sitting in the driver's seat.

Raoul looked back at John. "Do you want me to get the men from the back?"

John nodded, "Yes, you stay in the driver's seat, but send them out after me." John exited the cab of the truck and casually walked over to inspect the gold, ignoring the two soldiers standing guard near the entrance.

The soldier's name tags read Sanchez and Diaz. John thought Sanchez looked a little old to be a corporal. He and Diaz appeared to be in good shape, but something about Sanchez's eyes disgusted John. Soulless, like a drug addict's eyes.

Sanchez and Diaz watched John suspiciously as he inspected the gold, but made no move to interfere. John thought ten pounds of gold was probably more than the two of them earned in ten years of soldiering.

John triggered his communication channel to Sam. "The gold is here. Raoul is letting Pedro and his men out where they can be seen."

The entrance to the stone headquarters building opened and Garcia stepped out, followed by Sam, Edmond and Pedro's family. John heard a cry of joy as Pedro raced ahead of his men to hug his family.

Spotlights from the surrounding roofs stabbed down to cover the open area. John felt nervously exposed, out in the open with all these people to protect. Only Raoul was currently safe in the truck.

Garcia stepped out into the light covering the open courtyard, and then turned back to Sam, "Take the gold and go. I see Pedro and his men are here. You can see he has been reunited with his family."

Sam picked up the third of a gold bar with his left hand, and then handed it to Pedro, "Lead them all back to the truck." He turned to Garcia, "Change of plans. I've delivered them here as promised, in exchange for the gold. However, they've all signed up for Sharper Security to represent them and provide protection, so we'll be handling their defense and any trial."

John could see Garcia turning red. More to the point, he could see the heavy weapons squads already setup on the surrounding roof tops, some weapons aimed down at the open area in front of the headquarters building, others at the truck.

Pedro nodded and started to lead his men and family back to the truck. Edmond also followed. A rooftop spotlight pursued them, keeping them in sight. John stayed with Sam, trying to watch all the rooftops at once, feeling his own pistol wasn't going to have much effect if this came to a firefight. He wished he was back in the truck.

Garcia motioned to the nearest rooftop squad. A burst of heavy automatic weapons fire cut the ground midway between Pedro's group and the truck. Pedro stopped them and looked back.

"You may be able to kill me, Sam, but shortly afterwards Pedro and his family will die. Now the tables are turned." Garcia looked pleased with himself. "I know you. You won't let that happen."

Sam flipped up the visor on his suit again, "We could win a fight, but there would be casualties on both sides, starting with you, but I agree, likely ending with Pedro's family. However, even if they remained behind, I'm sure you have a missile battery, or a tank, or something like that planned to take us out in the truck before we can leave La Raza Council."

Garcia grinned knowingly, "We have ourselves a stand-off. I'm not coming with you. Not when I have you all surrounded by my soldiers."

Then Sam dropped a verbal bomb, "That's why I'm staying."

What?!? John thought. Staying? This wasn't part of the original plan. Sam was going to stick him with the responsibility for everyone? John choked a little on the dust in the air.

Sam pulled John over to stand behind Garcia, "Cover him with your pistol for a moment. I need to get out of this suit." Sam proceeded to open up the suit and step out. Handing John his helmet, he exchanged it for John's pistol. "Take the suit. I'll have my glasses and phone to communicate with you. Once you get across the border, I'm going to surrender to Lieutenant Garcia here."

Garcia smiled again, "Edmond stays also. That sounds like a fair trade to me."

Sam appeared to think for a moment, "Very well. Edmond stays with me."

John knew Garcia believed that with Sam as his prisoner, he'd be able to get many concessions from Sharper Security, including recovering Shortee Tejada in exchange. "Sam, you don't have to do this. You're under no obligation to sacrifice yourself for our new clients. Anyway, I can stay and cover Garcia just as well as you can."

Sam shook his head, "My company, my responsibility. Besides, it's good business for recruiting new clients. When word gets out about this, we'll have all sorts of people wanting to sign up with Sharper Security."

Garcia spoke louder, so his soldiers would hear, "We have a deal. Let these others go."

John muttered, "Yeah, people being held by psychopaths in a cell will be falling all over themselves to sign up with Sharper Security to get them out." Not exactly the safest marketing plan. Dubiously, John stepped into Sam's stealth armor suit. He then walked out in the open and led Pedro's group back to the truck.

Sam stayed behind at the entrance, standing with Garcia as protection from snipers, ready to cut Garcia's spinal cord with a bullet at the first sign of an attack.

Edmond stood beside Sam, opposite Sanchez and Diaz standing guard at the entrance.

John didn't feel like he was ready for this sort of responsibility again, but with no choice he told Raoul to get them out of La Raza Council as quickly as possible, leaving Sam and Edmond behind in the gathering night.

Edmond stood next to Sam and Garcia, being sure to keep Sam between him and the two Policía La Raza soldiers guarding the building entrance. He didn't look forward to dealing with Sanchez and Diaz again, especially now that he'd almost escaped.

Sam stood behind Garcia. He seemed attentive to Garcia and the Policía La Raza guards surrounding the area, but focused on watching John and the truck on the video feed in his glasses.

Edmond wished to be on that truck, even if it led to prison. He rubbed his shoulder, and then one of the deeper bruises on his leg. Edmond admired Sam for sacrificing himself to ensure his people got out safely. He just wished Garcia hadn't insisted Edmond stay behind. He much preferred the possibility of the Sharper Security prison to being subjected to Sanchez and Diaz again.

Sam spoke to Garcia from behind the Policía La Raza Lieutenant, "They're on the freeway. Another thirty minutes and I won't need to hold you anymore."

Garcia responded, "As soon as you shoot me, these men will kill you. Why don't you just save us some time and give up now. You don't want to die."

"Of course I don't want to die, but if that's required to make sure my men get out safely, then I will. You could ensure your men captured or killed us all, but that would require you to die first. Somehow I don't see you making the same sacrifice."

Edmond started thinking about the position his adopted father Pierre was in because of Edmond's actions. At least he'd had the sense to flee instead of starting a war between Agence de Sécurité and Sharper Security. He'd done that much right. Suddenly his need for revenge against Evie didn't seem so important. Not as important as living to see Pierre again. Not as important as his dream to become a protector of the innocent. What a stupid obsession with revenge. He'd grown up a decade in a day.

Watching Sam reminded Edmond he'd had another possible focus for his life beyond revenge. Before he noticed Evie coming to Maricopa, Edmond was following Pierre's path, someone who kept people safe. Too bad he'd ruined it all. Ruined his life. He rubbed his other shoulder, wincing with the pain.

Thirty minutes later, Sam watched a video feed in his glasses as the truck with Raoul, John, Pedro and the others cleared the Policía La Raza border checkpoint on I-10. His right arm was starting to get tired from holding a gun on Garcia. The tension remaining in the air was palpable.

Half expecting Garcia's men to try something before the truck could get out of La Raza Council territory, Sam wasn't about to relax his right arm. He didn't put it past Garcia to do something stupid. Still, Garcia prepared a decent position here at Policía headquarters. Between the spotlights and the men with automatic weapons on the rooftops, Garcia's men certainly had control of the overall area.

Sam learned a long time ago not to attack where the enemy was strong. Wait for an opportunity to strike where they aren't expecting it, where they are weak. He filed that away as another lesson to remind John of later. Assuming there was a later, but he'd been in tough situations before.

Edmond had been standing thoughtfully for a while, occasionally rubbing one of his bruises. The kid looked like a mess. Garcia's soldiers had obviously worked him over. Pierre wasn't going to be happy, but Edmond had brought it on himself.

Sanchez, one of the guards at the nearby HQ building entrance, spoke up, "El Teniente, the truck is reported past the checkpoint."

Garcia slowly turned and looked at Sam, "Time for you to surrender. We will have many interesting discussions. Perhaps now you will reconsider Shortee Tejada's fate?"

Sam had known it wouldn't take long for word to arrive. He'd put this off as long as possible. No more point in delaying further, "I agreed to surrender." He ejected the magazine from his pistol and handed them both over to Garcia. "You will get better results if you adhere to the agreements regarding prisoners."

Garcia took the pistol and magazine, "You are no longer in a position to make demands. My men will give you a proper welcome and then we will talk about Councilmember Tejada's son." He slotted the magazine back into the pistol with a thud, and then pointed it at Sam. "Now you are my prisoner. Edmond has already had a taste. Welcome back."

Sanchez and Diaz had seen the exchange and were already coming over to take the prisoners. With their rifles slung over their backs, the two soldiers openly carried black steel batons.

"We're coming." Sam said to them, trying to pre-empt an immediate attack. He used his right arm to pull Edmond towards the building entrance, keenly aware of all the Policía La Raza soldiers still surrounding them, "No need to do anything hasty."

Sam and Edmond walked towards the building entrance, closing the distance to the two guards. Sam focused on the nearest guard, Sanchez. As they approached, time slowed for Sam as he watched Sanchez's right arm start to pull back, and then swing forward with the baton extended.

This was going to hurt. At best. A strike to his head could also kill. To his shoulder socket, could disable. Surrounded by Policía La Raza, Sam couldn't fight back and win.

Sam blocked the baton swinging towards his head with his left forearm. Pain and shock radiated from the impact. Involuntarily, he sucked in his breath. Ouch, that hurt, Sam understated to himself, trying to stay on top of the shock.

When Sam collapsed to his knees, and then to the ground on his right side, cradling his left forearm, Sanchez seemed satisfied.

Edmond was horrified by seeing Sam hit the ground, taking an involuntary step back as Diaz approached him. Diaz just grabbed Edmond's left arm and roughly pulled him towards the entrance, "Let's go talk about staying in your place, gavacho."

Garcia smiled, "Soften them up. I will come negotiate with Sam once I've sent the rest of the company back to barracks. A fine night."

"Come on." Sanchez said to Sam, "You said you were coming."

Sam struggled to his feet, pain and shock on his face as he held his left forearm in his right hand. He staggered in shock toward the entrance, the pain radiating again with the jolt of each step.

Diaz led the way with Edmond. Edmond seemed to know where they were going and didn't resist his captor.

Sanchez roughly pushed Sam on the back through the doorway, heedless of his broken forearm. "Hurry up. I want to get some sleep tonight."

Sam kept on his feet and ahead of Sanchez. He could hear Garcia behind him shouting orders, dismissing his other men, sending them back to their barracks. He followed Edmond and Diaz.

Diaz slung his rifle off his back and set it in a rack in the entrance hallway. He led them into a nearby ground floor office. Sanchez's office. Edmond flinched subconsciously as he saw for certain where they were headed. Diaz stepped into the bare office and to one side of the doorway.

Edmond paused at the entrance, and then walked across the office to the wall opposite the doorway. He'd been hoping to be taken directly back to the cellar. Edmond's delay was enough to force Sam to stutter-step and pause.

Sanchez prodded Sam in the back harshly with his baton, "Keep moving."

Sam walked into the office and followed Edmond across to the other side. He turned to face their captors.

Sanchez placed his own rifle into the hallway rack, stepped into the office and closed the door. "This way the sound doesn't travel too far."

Sam looked around the sparsely furnished office. He held his left arm in towards his body, not needing to feign the pain he felt. Every movement of his broken forearm hurt, but he knew he needed to survive the next few minutes.

Diaz hung back by the closed door. Sanchez strut over to the prisoners with his baton held out from his right side.

Sam used his good right arm to push Edmond away from him along the wall. He knew he needed the room. Sam took one step toward Sanchez, his left foot forward, "Please don't do this. You don't have to do this." He spoke in a calm and level voice.

Sanchez's weight shifted to his right foot. His arm and baton went back in preparation to strike.

Sam moved forward quickly. Moved to get inside the reach of Sanchez's baton. Already halfway to Sanchez.

Sanchez also moved forward. Based on his experience, he expected to have to chase Sam a little. To get close enough to strike Sam at the edge of his baton's range. To trap him in the confined space of the office. The last thing Sanchez expected was a man with only one good arm to come towards him. Sam's movement didn't register immediately.

As the arm holding the baton came forward, Sam pivoted his body to the left, bringing his right arm and leg forward. He grabbed Sanchez's right wrist. The wrist holding the baton. Sam continued his circular movement. The combination of Sanchez's forward momentum with the baton and Sam's circular movement threw Sanchez forward.

Sanchez was rotated in the air onto his back. He landed heavily.

Sam landed on Sanchez with almost his full weight behind his right elbow. A right elbow positioned to crush Sanchez's windpipe.

Sanchez forgot about anything but trying to breathe. He lay on his back and struggled for air.

Sam grabbed up the baton as Sanchez released it. He struggled to stand and turn in time, knowing Diaz could already be swinging. Pain radiated from his left forearm. He still needed to protect that forearm.

Diaz approached cautiously. He held his baton carefully. He had seen Sanchez taken down, but the outcome wasn't clear to him yet. He was used to fighting with helpless prisoners, not dangerous men.

Sam extended his right leg and arm towards Diaz, holding the baton like a fencer, protecting his left arm from reach. "Stay back" he hissed to Edmond as he shuffled forward and to the right.

Diaz knew he was bigger. Likely stronger. Sam was hurt. He'd surprised them, but he still couldn't use his left arm. Diaz cautiously moved forward, trying to force Sam towards the corner of the room Edmond was hiding in.

Sam shuffled forward with his feet close together, weight barely on his back foot.

Diaz stood more open, facing him like a boxer with a club in his right hand. He held the baton close to his chest, looking for an opportunity.

As Diaz tried to crowd him, Sam mentally estimated the distance, making slight adjustments in how far apart they stood.

Sam lunged forward. He pushed with his left foot, reaching with the baton in his right arm. Stabbing slightly downward. Hitting Diaz's left leg just outside and above the knee. Jabbing into the bundle of nerves there.

Diaz's left leg went numb and started to collapse. As he fell, he managed to swing his baton and hit Sam in the chest. The impact wasn't as hard as the break in his left forearm, but Sam knew he'd feel it once the adrenaline wore off. Might have a broken rib or two.

Lying on the floor, Diaz tried to push himself up on his right leg.

Sam used his baton to sweep Diaz's right leg out from beneath him. He followed it up with a solid rap on Diaz's wrist, knocking the baton free from the fallen man. "You sure you want to continue this fight? Sanchez is already out."

Diaz tried to stand again. Sam gave him a carefully calculated knock above the ear with his baton. Fortunately, it was enough to knock Diaz out without killing him. Head blows could be risky.

"Edmond, get Sanchez's uniform on. We need to get out of here quickly."

Putting the larger Policia La Raza uniforms on over their own clothing, Edmond and Sam quickly dressed.

"Will they live?" Edmond asked.

"Likely, if someone discovers them soon." Sam looked at Edmond curiously, wondering how he'd respond. "Sanchez may end up with a little more brain damage. Probably suck wind through a tube the rest of his life."

"They don't deserve to live." Edmond rubbed his shoulder. "I could kill them right now and they'd never do this to anyone again."

"You're right, but to kill is a hard thing. It affects you. Especially if you don't *have* to do it. You don't deserve that sort of punishment. They aren't a threat. It doesn't have to be done right now. Just leave them."

"Alright." With that word, Edmond put a little more of his past behind him.

Sam fished a set of keys out of his right pocket and tossed them to Edmond, "You can drive. My left arm is starting to hurt again. Just walk out to the car. Walk normally. Look like you belong. Feel like you can blend in with that uniform. Just get in the car and drive off, just like you've done a thousand times before. No one will pay any attention. I'll be right next to you."

Edmond opened the office door and strode out as if he belonged. Sam followed him through the hallway, out the entrance, across the open space to the black Camaro parked in the lot. Quietly, they got in and drove to the gate.

With no alarm, the guard at the gate had no reason to try to stop a pair of soldiers in Policía uniform from leaving. Sam waved with his right arm as they passed out on to the road.

"Man I wish I had a splint." Sam said as the Camaro hit a pothole. "Turn left onto the freeway and show me how fast this Camaro will go. Don't stop for anything."

"Am I driving too rough? I think I saw a first aid kit back in the cellar. We could go back and see if they have a splint?" Edmond seemed relieved to be out of Policía La Raza hands.

"Thanks for the offer, but I'll just hold on until we get somewhere a little quieter. We have maybe ten minutes before those two are discovered and we need to be at least on the North side of Tucson by then. After that, it'll depend on how fast word gets to Garcia and how long it takes them to realize your car is gone."

Old I-10 Freeway, North of La Raza Council

Almost Midnight

Raoul sat at the wheel of the truck parked northbound on the shoulder of I-10. Just north of Marana, they were past the areas people lived and out where the desert started in earnest.

John had been talking to Sam for the last thirty minutes. "They'll be here soon. Start us moving north slowly. Be ready to move behind them once they pass us. This isn't over yet."

Raoul had heard the same information from Sam over the truck's communication system, but he figured John was reassured by confirming it anyway. Raoul started the big diesel engine up and began slowly rolling north along the shoulder, ready to accelerate when needed.

John stood and made his way into the back with the control stations.

Even though he expected it, the rumble from the roof of the truck opening up surprised Raoul. He glanced at a camera feed covering the roof and saw a missile launcher facing back to the south, angled ready to fire.

Sam's voice came over the sound system again, "John, I'm sending coordinates of a fence line right beside the border control station. I need one high explosive missile targeted there to make a hole for us. Launch in 30 seconds."

"Marking the current time. Launching one high explosive missile at the provided coordinates in 30 seconds, aye." Edmond responded.

Raoul heard the brief roar of a rocket engine as a missile fired out of the rooftop launcher.

"One high explosive missile away." John said.

Raoul heard a distant boom as the missile exploded on impact.

"Good shot. Made a nice hole in the fence line for us to bypass the border checkpoint. Probably woke the neighbors up, so be prepared to provide air cover." Sam sounded pleased.

"Tracking two aerial drones on radar. Both have diverted this direction. Not sure if they're armed or not." John reported.

"We've successfully bypassed the border station and are back on the freeway. We'll be there soon. Ask Pedro to dig through the first aid kit in the back of the truck and find a splint. We can stop and talk once we're well clear."

As Edmond and Sam approached them in a black Camaro, John launched four surface to air missiles at targets in the sky only he could see on radar.

Raoul had to floor the accelerator to speed up as the black Camaro passed them on the freeway. Raoul pulled out into the slow lane as he accelerated, thankful the freeway was quiet with traffic at this time of year.

Hearing explosions, Raoul could see two fireballs in the air behind them. Madre de Dios! He hadn't signed up to drive in a war.

"Got them!" John shouted from the back. "I doubt Policia La Raza will send any more drones after us. Those suckers are expensive."

"Good job. Let's stop in Picacho Pass on the way home. Maybe get some ice cream and splint this broken arm. You know the westernmost battle of the civil war was fought there? I love road trips." Sam sounded to Raoul like he was still in pain, but obviously relieved to be out of La Raza Council.

The black Camaro slowed slightly to allow the truck to follow close behind and provide protection to them both. Raoul was just happy to be finally headed north and away from La Raza Council. Maybe he could drop this truck off at the Sharper Security prison and still be home by the time the sun came up.

Chapter 6 - Day Six

Hidden Valley Road, Maricopa, Arizona Zone

Next Morning

Evie woke with a start. The prison infirmary bed felt cool. The morning sun shone in through a high up window on the east side. Early morning in the desert seemed to be the nicest time of day.

After a second, Evie realized what woke her. The paramedic bloke startled her awake as he hurried in, slamming open the door from the hallway. He was followed into the room by Sam and then John.

"I don't think you've fractured both bones in your forearm. It looks like just the ulna on the outside of your forearm, but I still need to get that arm imaged, make sure it's set correctly, and then put it in a proper splint." the paramedic said, a little too loudly. Evie winced at the interruption.

"I've had worse." Sam said as he followed the paramedic over to the imaging machine. "The swelling is already starting to go down."

The paramedic shook his head, "The swelling won't stabilize for a while, but we may be able to avoid surgery. I'll send the images I've taken to a specialist and we'll get a series of them over the next few days."

"The only reason your arm isn't a foot thick is because I made you ice it in the truck all the way from Picacho Pass." John added. "Besides, it still looks pretty swollen to me."

"Who asked you? We have Edmond's trial on the Rez starting in an hour and don't think for a second Judge Parkur is going to like us being late, even if he is your father. In fact, that makes him especially likely to make a big deal out of it." Sam seemed irritated by something, Evie thought. Maybe his broken arm?

"This will only take a few minutes." the paramedic interjected, "Then you can go back to ruining my work again. You know this is the second time you've broken your left forearm? We should probably be putting a steel plate in."

"Third. The first was before your time. Or was that my right arm? It's hard to keep track. Besides, I didn't break it, the other guy did. I just happened to be in the way at the time." Sam said.

"You blocked that baton with your forearm on purpose. Can't fool me, I heard all about it on the ride back. Make Garcia relax his guard while keeping Sanchez from bashing your head in. You could have blocked his arm instead, if you'd wanted to." John seemed upset at being left out of the argument, even a little.

"I'm looking at the pictures. Only evidence of two fractures total on this arm. Alright, flip it over." the paramedic said as he finished fiddling on the real-time imager and looking at the resulting pictures, "I need to get one from the other side to make sure everything is properly aligned. Later, we'll see what the specialist says."

Evie decided this was a good time to interrupt. This was more interesting than faffing about watching the telly all day, "You sent me a message that you'd recovered Edmond from La Raza, but what's this thing about a trial?"

Sam was busy grimacing at the paramedic, so John looked over at Evie and replied, "Justice moves quickly and efficiently when everything is this cut and dried. On the way home, Sharper Security officially found Edmond guilty of destruction of your property, assault, battery and attempted murder. Pierre, at Agence de Sécurité, didn't dispute most of the charges, but he countered by saying it was a pre-existing condition and you aren't covered for that, so we have no right to try Edmond in the matter. He also doesn't agree with the attempted murder charge."

"Just a simple fracture. One bone. Good alignment. Probably won't take long to heal, although you aren't getting any younger." The paramedic let Sam go and wandered over to a shelf to start pulling the makings of a new splint off it.

Sam rubbed his arm a little and then joined the conversation with Evie, "To speed things up, we all stipulated to most of the facts and agreed that per our arbitration agreements, Judge Parkur out on the Rez will make the final decision on appeal. He has all the evidence already. We sent it to him a couple of hours ago from the truck, so he's likely reviewed quite a bit. We'll have a hearing today. Finish up tonight, or tomorrow at the latest. Judge Parkur doesn't waste any time on non-essentials. Hopefully we can have this all behind us by tomorrow."

Evie felt cold. "When can I get out of here?"

"You can leave any time you want. Edmond is locked up in the prison pending transfer for the appeal on the Rez and he was acting alone. Do you have anywhere to go? There are plenty of hotels around, but you're also welcome to stay here. Either way, Sharper Security will take care of your housing until we can finish rebuilding your home." Sam added.

The paramedic said, "I still recommend you both get some rest, but I'm sure no one plans to listen to me about it."

"I'm listening." John said with a bright smile.

Evie sighed, "I don't need a child-minder. After the trial, I'll find a flat to rent. I saw an advert on the telly."

"I'm transporting Edmond over to the Rez in the prison van, but I'll send John to pick you up for the trial." Sam said.

"How long does it take? I'm not really dressed to go out yet." Evie asked.

"To get to the Rez Courthouse?" John replied, "With Sam driving, about 15 minutes, but I'll get you there in one piece, so more like half an hour. I'll help Sam get Edmond loaded up, then drop back by in thirty minutes to get you."

The paramedic finished wrapping Sam's forearm in a more permanent splint, "No impacts for a few weeks. You don't want to mess up the alignment before it starts healing. The painkiller in your system is non-drowsy, but I don't know how you plan to drive with this splint on."

Sam had an answer for that, as he seemed to have for everything, "Don't worry, the van's an automatic. I can drive with one arm."

With that, they all left, leaving Evie to try to get herself ready to leave in only thirty minutes. Don't they understand that some things take longer than that?

John stepped into dorm #4. Still the same grey metal sleeping racks scattered across the room, although he looked with more respect on the big hose nozzles up on the wall.

"Edmond. Time for your trial on the Rez." John said. Didn't Sam usually send a robot to get prisoners?

"Hey, the fish turned into a screw. You rat one of my homies out, ese? Looking to get on that gabacho warden's good side?" Shortee Tejada called out. Shortee was sitting at a table playing cards with three of his cronies, but the action paused when John arrived.

Edmond looked asleep on his rack, but John wasn't sure. Shortee was all the way across the room. Edmond was closer, but hadn't responded to John's entrance.

Standing up from his chair, Shortee walked toward John. His stride was deceptively casual, but John could see the tension underneath it. Had it only been a few days? It seemed like forever since John was here as a prisoner.

John looked over at one of the cameras and shook his head. He assumed Sam was monitoring the situation, alerted by one of his camera-feed watching expert systems.

Shortee casually leaned over next to his bed and slipped something into his hand. You could always make or trade for a shank in prison, John thought. The three cronies stood up and started belatedly following Shortee by casually filtering around the room towards John.

"Still haven't grown up, Shortee?" Edmond's voice came just as Shortee was about to pass by him. To all appearances, Edmond was relaxed, but his eyes were open now.

John started walking towards Shortee and Edmond. He was supposed to be in charge here now.

"Stay out of this and maybe when I deal with you later, it won't be so painful." Shortee said.

Edmond leaned over on his side in his bunk, facing Shortee. "Don't let these bruises fool you. I took you down at the Francisco Grande and I can do it again." Edmond sounded older and more confident than he looked.

While Shortee was glaring at Edmond, John stepped up next to them, "Don't worry about it, Edmond. Shortee's been hiding behind his name so long he thinks it makes him a bad man, rather than just a bad son."

The motion of Shortee's right arm towards John was fast. Anticipating the attack, Edmond's right hand was faster, grabbing Shortee's wrist and letting the momentum of the swinging arm help him to his feet.

Edmond grabbed Shortee where his neck and shoulder blade met with his left hand and twisted Shortee's right arm behind his back in a hammerlock. Edmond forced Shortee's hand higher up his back, toward his neck, forcing him to drop the sharpened metal bunk leg he'd been carrying.

"While I'm sure John would be happy to dance with you, he's here to pick me up. You don't want me to be late for my court date, do you?" Edmond's voice was level.

Shortee's followers started drifting back toward the card laden table.

John picked up the solid looking shank from the floor, "You can let him go. You don't have time for this and he obviously thinks he needs a weapon or some friends for backup. Apparently, you've deprived him of both. Without them he's a small man."

Edmond laughed at John's pun and shoved Shortee back toward the table he'd walked from, causing him to stumble and have to regain his balance. "You're right. No need to waste time on him. Let's go."

The two men turned to face the dorm's entrance, clearly unafraid to walk with their backs to Shortee.

"Maybe we should have put you in the infirmary for those bruises instead of leaving you in the general population." John said as they walked through the dorm room entrance.

"With Evie? Somehow I doubt that slipped Sam's consideration."

When they reached the garage, John dropped the shank into a handy trash can. "Sam's driving you, so wait here. I just realized I need to hit the head before leaving."

"Sure, no problem." Edmond said. He sounded unsure of why John trusted him to stay unguarded in a garage full of escape vehicles.

"You came back with Sam when he had a broken arm. I'm sure you aren't planning to take off now. Besides, knowing Sam, you couldn't get the garage door open or one of those vehicles started without some computer system signing off on it."

"True. I hope he still has the keys to my Camaro."

Seed Farm Road, Sacaton, Arizona Zone

Noon

Pierre stepped into the marble-floored hallway outside Judge Parkur's Gila River Reservation courtroom. After the morning court session, he'd just had time to go down the street for some fry bread and black beans. It wasn't French cuisine, but made fresh it wasn't bad. After the lunch break, court was scheduled to resume with Edmond's testimony about the attempted murder charge.

Sam leaned up against the opposite wall, dressed in shorts even for court. Probably told the Judge he wasn't able to change clothing because of the big splint on his arm.

"You trained that kid well. I watched him handle Shortee Tejada again this morning. It looked like there might be trouble, nothing John wouldn't have handled, but he calmed things down." Sam said.

"I don't like him in prison. Many of those men were put there by Agence de Sécurité." Pierre said. Former law enforcement officers usually had a difficult time in prison.

"I did what I had to. No hard feelings?" Sam asked.

"No, Sam. He is better there than in La Raza Council. Just this morning, Edmond told me what happened. Thank you for getting him out of there. How is your arm?"

"It's been better and worse before. If they put it in a cast, I'll have you sign it." Sam looked concerned for Pierre. "Trust in Judge Parkur. He seems to have a knack for making these sorts of things come out right."

"Tu connais la musique. You know the music. Let us go in. They will be starting once more soon." Pierre said as he walked past Sam towards the courtroom double-doors. He hoped Sam was right about Judge Parkur, but he was afraid Edmond was in more trouble than he could escape.

Sam followed Pierre into the courtroom. Judge Parkur wasn't yet back up on the raised dark wood desk called a "bench". As far as Pierre could tell, it was just a normal desk with the Gila River Reservation flag behind it. Things weren't so formal at Agence de Sécurité, but he remembered worse back in France.

Pierre and Sam went to sit at opposite tables, Sam for the prosecution and Pierre for the defense. Pierre felt sure that the facts were on Edmond's side, but you could never be too confident with your son's future at stake.

Evie sat in the spectator area at the back of the courtroom. All of her testimony had been recorded and presented to Judge Parkur before any of this began. Pierre hadn't challenged any of it, nor demanded to cross-examine her, so she was allowed to observe the proceedings.

John, the judge's son, sat next to Evie. Pierre believed that wouldn't influence the judge, but he also wasn't about to make a fuss about it in a way that made Judge Parkur lose face without any benefit.

A Reservation Police Officer brought Edmond back into the court and up to the witness stand to continue his testimony. What Sam couldn't give the judge as pre-recorded evidence was Edmond himself. Sam had just acquired him from Policía La Raza late last night.

The bailiff commanded, "All Rise." A pause to let the Judge walk in and take his chair. "Gila River Appeals Court, the Honorable Judge Parkur presiding."

"Please be seated." Judge Parkur waved everyone back down, "We were in the middle of testimony when the court recessed for lunch. Let the record show that the defendant is still sworn and giving testimony. As previously agreed and in the interests of time, let's keep this fairly informal, if possible. Pierre, you may continue your questioning."

Pierre thought Judge Parkur liked to hear himself speak, even if he was keeping things informal for Sam and Pierre. "Edmond, we were discussing the alleged attempted murder with a sniper rifle a few days ago. When you fired your shot, what were you aiming at?"

Edmond cleared his throat, "A sign. I aimed for a message I stuck on the street name sign."

"Did you hit what you aimed at?"

"Yes. I'm a good shot. Should be, you made me practice every week."

Pierre smiled, "I did. When is ze last time you missed something you were aiming a stabilized sniper rifle at?"

Edmond frowned, "I'm not sure... maybe a few years ago?"

"That's good enough. To be clear, you weren't aiming at any person? Just a sign?"

"Yes. I hit it, too."

Pierre nodded, "Your Honor, I've transmitted an image of ze sign-post in question previously to you and Mr. Harper. You'll see a bullet hole in ze sign, right through a paper stuck on top of the road sign. The paper reads, 'This could be you'."

Judge Parkur nodded, "We have the image. Sam, any objection?"

Sam stood briefly, "No, Your Honor. The image matches what was found at the scene."

"Thank you." Pierre continued, turning back towards Edmond, "John Parkur reported only hearing one shot fired that day. Did you only fire that one shot?"

"Yes."

"Why shoot? What was your purpose?"

"I just wanted to scare her. Wanted her to feel a little of the hurt I felt at never knowing my parents. My real parents, I mean. I can see now that was stupid."

"Thank you Edmond. Sam, your witness." Pierre sat down, feeling he'd made his points."

Sam stood, "Why was it stupid, Edmond?"

Edmond's hands shook a little. He seemed to be fighting back tears, "Nothing will get my parents back. I know that. I wanted to get revenge, but all I did was get myself into trouble over her. She's not worth it. I need to stick to my first plans. Become a protector like Pierre. As I said, it was stupid. I'm still not sure what came over me. Obsession, I guess. After all those years of thinking about my parents, wishing I knew them. Mad at Evie for killing them. Then she moved into town and I started watching her with the drones. I was obsessed with revenge."

"Obsessed enough to try and kill her? To get even?" Sam asked.

Edmond paused to think for a second. "Maybe eventually, but I didn't. I was just trying to scare her that day. That's all. Just scare her."

"No further questions, Your Honor." Sam said.

"Pierre?" Judge Parkur inquired.

"Nothing further, Your Honor." Pierre replied. He still wasn't sure he shouldn't have assigned someone else to defend his son, especially because he knew Evie from his past and was probably part of the reason for Edmond's obsession.

"I will review the provided evidence and testimony and notify you of my verdict. This court is adjourned."

Hidden Valley Road, Maricopa, Arizona Zone

Late afternoon

Pedro stood in Sam's office. They'd been discussing the future of his family and the soldiers that followed him in signing up with Sharper Security.

Sam seemed to notice something in his glasses. He held up a hand to interrupt his conversation with Pedro, "You may want to hear this, so I'll put it on the big screen there, but please stay quiet and out of camera range."

Pedro backed away from Sam's desk a little and turned to see the screen Sam was gesturing toward.

El Jefe appeared on the screen with his own office in the background, "Sam Harper. You keep meddling in my affairs."

"Is that the way to greet someone who has known you for so long? It is just as good to see you again. You must give my greeting to Lieutenant Garcia as well." Sam seemed amused.

"You left me a message. Said we needed to speak. So speak." El Jefe went straight to the point.

"I was able to settle the incident of your men trespassing with Garcia, but after that I received a broken arm... " Sam raised his splint, "... and was assaulted and illegally detained by your men without any sort of charge."

"That was all Garcia's doing. Policía La Raza disclaims any responsibility for any unfortunate occurrences while you were visiting."

"Strange, they were all wearing Policía uniforms at the time and the incidents took place in your headquarters. I believe that makes you liable. We recently came so close to an open war. We wouldn't want to start provoking incidents again, would we? I might have to put the case before one of my underwriters and see what they think."

El Jefe blustered, "As I said, all was Garcia's responsibility. As you note, the incidents took place at Policía La Raza headquarters and under our jurisdiction. As a member of La Raza Council, Garcia is ours to punish for any actions taken under our jurisdiction. We have arrested the men responsible for the incident."

"At least some of them. As the victim and a member of Sharper Security, compensation must still be provided. Otherwise, Sharper Security will be forced to demand compensation rather more strenuously."

Pedro thought el Jefe was trapped. If he didn't pay up, the underwriters would get involved and he might start a war he wouldn't win. If he paid Sam, he'd look weak. If he gave Garcia to Sharper Security, he'd look even weaker.

El Jefe didn't even stop to consider, meaning he'd decided before returning Sam's call, "In the interests of showing we do not condone the treatment of visitors you received, Policía La Raza will pay for your medical bills and something suitable for any lost work time."

Sam shook his head, "For me, you will pay the statutory damages for an assault, a broken arm in the furtherance of that assault and for unlawful restraint. Nothing less. You know that is what the underwriters will decide. Save us all some time and don't push an issue you're bound to lose."

"In the interest of fairness and being a good neighbor, we will pay your damages. We just want to put the whole incident behind us." El Jefe didn't look happy to Pedro, nor interested in fairness.

"You will also pay statutory damages for Edmond's torture and for his unlawful restraint. I presume you know how high standard damages for torture are in order to discourage the practice." Sam added.

El Jefe took one more shot, "Edmond was apprehended as a criminal, wanted by Sharper Security. Certainly you should be paying Policía La Raza for turning him over to you."

"Garcia initially turned Edmond over to me based on a verbal agreement we made. I kept my part of that agreement. I happen to have recorded it with full video, if you need a copy. The agreement was made in your headquarters. He was tortured illegally, not pursuant to law. Also, he was restrained after he had been released to my custody, at the same time I was illegally restrained. As it happens, I have all of that recorded as well. Don't you just love modern technology?"

El Jefe sighed, "Very well. We will pay."

"Good. You will pay the damages for Edmond into a fund I've setup for his victim here. It will be used to restore the damage he's responsible for. I will send you two contracts to execute. Is there anything else we need to discuss?" Sam smiled again, but Pedro could see a hidden intensity behind the smile. Now el Jefe knew what Pedro felt when faced by a row of anti-personnel mines and nowhere to hide.

"Until next time." El Jefe still put a threat into his voice before disconnecting.

With the call over, Pedro stepped forward again, "I am a poor man, but I have been a soldier. You said my family could stay here, but that you had work for me and my men?"

"You have been a thug, supporting men who live off other people's sweat. I will make you and your men into soldiers. Protectors of people instead of their oppressors. You make good decisions quickly. We can use that." Sam replied, "I've been giving you and your men some thought. I believe it's time to open up a more southern market for Sharper Security. I'd like you to start a branch in Tucson. You and your men know the area, know the people, and have many friends there. I've been meaning to expand again. Your family, and the family of anyone you feel may be in immediate danger, may stay here where they will be easier to protect. At least at first."

Pedro was stunned, "Return to La Raza Council, this time working for Sharper Security?"

"You need a job, don't you? I mean, you can go get a job at some other security outfit. Some of the ones in Chandler, Tempe or Phoenix are a little less risky. If you have other skills, you can do whatever someone will pay you for, up here. Don't misunderstand. I'm looking for willing volunteers. People who understand what is at stake."

"I am unsure, Señor. I must speak with mi esposa, mi corazón." My wife, my heart.

Sam made it sound like a good opportunity. "Give it some thought. Things have settled down around here and it's time Sharper Security expanded. Certainly, the people in Tucson don't seem to realize they have a choice besides those city council members that took over after the Big Split. Unlike trying to expand farther north, where there are lots of established sovereign security companies fighting for customers, Tucson should be easy competition, once the people living there realize they really have a choice. The hardest part will be getting started, but you and your men, with your local knowledge of the criminals and the powers that be, will be a good start."

"I will think on this. Thank you for the chance, the opportunity."

Tejada Copper Mine, Tucson, La Raza Council

Late afternoon

Garcia wanted desperately to wipe the sweat from his face. The heavy rubber gloves and his protective face mask wouldn't let him. He kept pushing the pump down and then letting the similarly masked figure on the other side push it back up.

Push, rest and breathe, push again. Garcia stood drenched in sweat. It pooled in his thick rubber boots and ran down the inside of his PVC plastic suit.

This morning, Garcia thought he'd get out of the hottest work for a while. The shift foreman didn't have protective suits round enough to fit Garcia in the dressing room of the copper mine.

Garcia believed the foreman's supervisor had made it clear Garcia was to be assigned to the hardest work. Why else would the foreman delay the start of work for everyone in order to go retrieve a larger suit from somewhere else?

Abandoned by the previous owners during the Big Split, the copper mine had been taken over by La Raza Council. Pieces of the previous mine automation missing or out of order, they'd substituted prisoners for parts of the copper recovery process.

The process involved pumping acid down a borehole in the desert to the copper deposits, and then pumping the resulting dissolved copper and acid back up another borehole.

New boreholes were still mostly drilled by the one remaining piece of heavy machinery, but the pumps used to move the acid had broken down years before.

Garcia's new job was to push down one side of a teeter-totter style hand pump. Another prisoner would push down the other side, raising Garcia's side. The hand pumps weren't ideally suited for the task and had a nasty tendency to squirt acid out unexpectedly on those doing the pumping. Hence, the protective suits.

The actual pumping was hard enough. Garcia was required by the shift foreman to keep up with the man on the other side of the hand pump.

La Raza Council needed the hard income the copper mine brought. The pumps were run 24 hours a day, with breaks taken only for shift changes and maintenance.

As a new and disfavored prisoner with no means of bribing the foreman, Garcia was assigned to the day shift. Without some shade, the daytime pumpers would die. Without the suit, temperatures reached 110-120 degrees during summer afternoons. With shade, temperatures inside the suit reached 120+ degrees as soon as the pumper started work in the morning, hotter as the day went on.

"Don't worry about it." the foreman had said when handing Garcia his new, larger suit, "We'll melt those pounds off you and have you in a regular size suit within a few weeks."

Then the foreman had laughed. "Assuming you last that long in the sun." Garcia no longer found dark humor funny.

Hidden Valley Road, Maricopa, Arizona Zone

Late afternoon

Sam watched Pedro leave his office. He was sure that once Pedro and his wife thought about it, they'd decide they had lots of friends and some extended family in La Raza Council that they didn't want to leave behind. He already knew just where he wanted them to start, but that was for another week. At this point, Sam could really use a rest.

John had taken Evie to a hotel after court was out. Sam had told him to go somewhere nice. It was good to have a reputation for taking care of your customers, even if Evie wasn't the ideal client.

Sam checked the digital clock in the corner of his glasses. Time for a teleconference with Judge Parkur and Pierre to hear the results. He made sure John had connected a listen-only feed for Evie and then made his own connection. So much more convenient than traveling down in person. Edmond would also be listening from his jail cell on the Rez. Sam imagined Pierre would be with his adopted son instead of back at the Agence de Sécurité office.

Judge Parkur came on the screen from his court, ready to announce the verdict, "In the matter of Agence de Sécurité v. Sharper Security, appeal of the Sharper Security findings against a member of Agence de Sécurité …"

Sam listened as the specific charges and issues for appeal were read. The appeal included the ultimate liability of Edmond to Sharper Security for his actions, Sharper Security's representation of Evie and the sentence Edmond received.

Judge Parkur continued with his judgment, "As Evie is responsible for the negligent homicide of Edmond's parents, as well as making the defendant homeless, that pre-existing condition releases her from personal protection by Sharper Security according to their contract. Thus, other than the property damage issues, this becomes a matter of only Agence de Sécurité jurisdiction and judgment. The Agence de Sécurité judgment on the personal matters, including innocence of the charge of attempted murder, is upheld."

Not surprised as the judge continued, Sam wondered how Evie would take the results. He'd known that if Edmond was responsible for the harassment and the story about Evie killing his parents held up, Sharper Security really had no business protecting her from him. A criminal couldn't be allowed to pay for the personal protection of one sovereign security company against the victim of the criminal's crimes.

As the next of kin for his murdered parents and a victim of the bombing in his own right, Edmond had three good claims against Evie. No sovereign immunity existed in Arizona Zone. Sharper Security's responsibility to their customers was to protect them under an assumption of innocence until a court found otherwise. Sam typically took it farther, giving his customers all the benefit of the doubt as long as possible.

"As for the matter of property damage, Edmond is guilty of damaging a number of autocabs as well as a home under the jurisdiction of Sharper Security. The defendant's beating and torture by Policía La Raza while holding him for these crimes is sufficient punishment and their payment to a fund to recompense him will cover restitution to pay for the actual property damage. Thus, the sentence of time served and financial restitution is appropriate. The defendant is ordered immediately released. This court stands adjourned."

Sam nodded to himself. The ruling as he'd expected. He'd have to tell Maria about it all. Ask her to help out a bit more with Pedro and his family.

Chapter 7 - Day Seven

Gila Bend Highway, Casa Grande, Arizona Zone

Sunrise

Evie stepped out to an open exterior walkway connecting the penthouse suites on the ninth floor. The walkway felt like a concrete ledge overhanging a cliff. Even with the railing, the trip down the exposed walkway to the elevators frightened her. The rising sun shone in her face as she walked. Heights were never her strong suit.

She found the Pat Boone Suite of the Francisco Grande Hotel very charming and quaint, with brand new 1960's décor. For some reason, her room's balcony overlooking the golf course, playing fields and the baseball bat shaped pool didn't frighten her in the same way.

The elevator down to the lobby was more solid than the outside walkway. Enclosed. The elevator and the lobby kept the hotel's theme, looking brand new, with décor from at least 70 years ago. She could imagine herself walking around a corner to find John Wayne standing there.

Pushing the button for the lobby, Evie knew she'd have a wait. Well maintained and quiet, the elevator relied on older technology. On her way down, she marveled over the plush red on the walls. They really knew how to be luxurious in the last century.

Evie stepped out of the elevator and found Edmond waiting for her.

Edmond knew he could kill Evie.

The hotel contracted for protection with Agence de Sécurité. Part of his normal responsibilities when working around the corner on Cowtown road was to respond to calls at the Francisco Grande.

No one would stop him.

Edmond always liked visiting the Francisco Grande. Walking through the lobby or the restaurants, he felt he'd gone to a different world. A place where the past met the present. A refuge of solitude and protection.

A place where he excised any interruption, any disruption.

Evie stood in the entrance of the elevator, preventing the doors from closing. A pair of three foot tall giant clay pots flanked the elevator doors with cacti. Evie wore a black dress with pretensions of youth.

Edmond looked at Evie and saw fear in her eyes.

Evie watched Edmond's left hand grasp the large silver cross around his neck. His right hand fell to the butt of his holstered pistol. She felt her knee shake. Had an urge to run.

Edmond just stood there, staring at her, ripening bruises evident on his face and arms.

"I'm sorry." Evie said. "I was young. I didn't take my job seriously enough. It was a lark."

Edmond didn't respond. He just stood there, fingering his pistol.

"I'm sorry about your parents, Edmond, but it's been eighteen years."

Edmond replied, "Eighteen years and seven days." He thought of his parents, of the stories Pierre told him, trying to explain to a child what had happened. Why he missed them.

He could avenge them now. He saw Evie's frightened eyes stare at his neck, then at the pistol holster attached to his belt.

"That's right", he said, "I have everything back now. I'm not going to throw it away again."

Edmond knew he could kill her right now without *legal* consequence. Evie knew it, too. Edmond thought back to what Sam told him about killing.

"I won't kill you. You should be grateful for those seven days. They just saved your life."

It didn't matter if she apologized. Edmond owned a new life now. One not ruled by the ruins in his past.

"Mine too." Edmond added. The man turned and walked outside to patrol the hotel grounds.

*** **The End** ***

For a complete list of currently available Sharper Security books and short stories, plus notification of future related publications, please send an email to NotifyMe@SharperSecurity.com.

To find author's notes about this book and other books and short stories in the series, please visit us at SharperSecurity.com.